Also by O. R. Melling

The Druid's Tune
The Singing Stone
My Blue Country

The Chronicles of Faerie
The Hunter's Moon
The Summer King

Adult Fiction
Falling Out of Time

THE
LIGHT-BEARER'S DAUGHTER

BOOK THREE IN
THE CHRONICLES OF FAERIE

O.R. MELLING

PENGUIN BOOKS

PENGUIN BOOKS
PUBLISHED BY THE PENGUIN GROUP
Penguin Books Canada Ltd, 10 Alcorn Avenue, Toronto, Ontario, Canada M4V 3B2
Penguin Books Ltd, 27 Wrights Lane, London W8 5TZ, England
Penguin Putnam Inc., 375 Hudson Street, New York, New York 10014, U.S.A.
Penguin Books Australia Ltd, Ringwood, Victoria, Australia
Penguin Books (NZ) Ltd, CNR Rosedale and Airborne Roads, Albany,
Auckland 1310, New Zealand

Penguin Books Ltd, Registered Offices: Harmondsworth, Middlesex, England

First published 2001

1   3   5   7   9   10   8   6   4   2

*Publisher's note: This book is a work of fiction. Names, characters, places and incidents either
are the product of the author's imagination or are used fictitiously, and any resemblance to
actual persons living or dead, events, or locales is entirely coincidental.*

Manufactured in Canada

CANADIAN CATALOGUING IN PUBLICATION DATA

Melling, O.R.
The light-bearer's daughter
(The chronicles of Faerie; 3.)

ISBN 0-14-100459-2
I. Title. II. Series: Melling, O. R. Chronicles of Faerie; 3.

PS8576.E463L53 2001   jC813'.54   C00-932478-X
PZ7.M51625Li 2001

Visit Penguin Canada's website at **www.penguin.ca**

For
my mother and my daughter

Acknowledgements

Many thanks to: Findabhair ní Fhaoláin and Amanda Walton Terry of Wolfe Tone Square, my inspirations for Dana; Marian Richardson, who took me on journeys through the mountains; Tony Hall, who introduced me to the eco-warriors in the Glen of the Downs; Ger McGrath for racing me up Lugnaquillia; Michael Scott for so many things I can't list them but certainly the computer; Billy Duffin for looking after my house; Nena Hardie, fellow traveller amongst the megaliths and dear host in Toronto; Heather Brown, a light that led me out of the darkness; dear friends Maura Walsh and Martina Brady for moral support; the wonderful staff at the Tyrone Guthrie Centre for the Arts—Regina Doyle, Doreen Burns, Theresa Rudden and Lavina McAdoo; Rita Morrissey and Michael Kelleher of the Bray Library; Gearóidín ní Bhaoill for checking my Irish; editors Meg Masters and Barbara Berson and all at Penguin Canada; agents Lynn and David Bennett of Transatlantic Literary Inc.; *Na Daoine Maithe*, as always, for their generous permission and assistance; and *in memoriam*, sweet Millie, our little white rabbit.

Thanks are also due to:

Anne Fitzpatrick of Powerscourt House, Wicklow County Council, the Bray Urban District Council, the Irish

Acknowledgements

Arts Council for an Aer Lingus Artsflight, and the Cultural
Relations Committee of the Department of Foreign Affairs
(Ireland).

AUTHOR'S NOTE

CHAPTERS SIXTEEN AND Seventeen were greatly inspired by Glendalough—*A Celtic Pilgrimage* by Michael Rodgers and Marcus Losack (Columba Press, Ireland, and Morehouse Publishing, United States).

There are various quotes throughout the book from the King James Version of the Bible, the most notable being on page 104 (from Jeremiah 6:16) and page 108 (from Psalm 61:1–3).

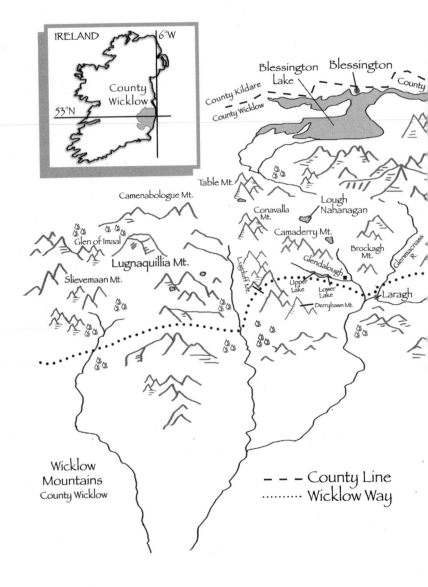

THE

LIGHT-BEARER'S DAUGHTER

BOOK THREE IN
THE CHRONICLES OF FAERIE

Chapter One

A SHADOW MOVED ACROSS the sky, obscuring the sun. The green light of the forest darkened. Squirrels sat up in their dreys, alert. The chirr of insects ceased. A fox stopped in its tracks, hair bristling, nose to the air. The stench was foul. A rabbit thumped the ground. *Warning. Danger.* All held their breath as they awaited catastrophe.

It was only for a moment, but it was a moment of pure terror. The threat of extinction. A moment in which the heart was seized, the throat gripped, the breath blocked.

Then the shadow passed.

She ran through the woods like one who was hunted. The earth was cool and damp beneath her bare feet. She wore a green kirtle with a yellow surcoat. Her hair was wreathed with white blossoms. Pressing her ear to the bole of an oak, she closed her eyes to listen. The murmur of life calmed her.

She smiled, called upwards into the leaves quivering in the sunlight.

Tá grian gheal an tsamhraidh ag damhsa ar mo theach.
The summer sun is dancing on the roof of my house.

The wind whistled and sang as it took up her words and cast them about like a summons. The skirr of bird wings sounded overhead. Rooks and ravens lighted in the branches. Smaller creatures gathered at her feet, gently pawing the hem of her skirt.

Her look was grave.

"The King and I fear for the Summer Land."

They let out little cries. Some went mute with fright.

She kept her voice firm.

"Be of good courage. We are not alone. Keep watch for the messenger and help her on her way."

From the living-room window, Gabriel watched his daughter play football in the street. Tall and lanky, dark curls bouncing on her shoulders, Dana wove in and out of the other children to kick the ball ahead of her. The goalpost was a crack in the road. If she got the ball over it and didn't trip and split her head, she won. Her teammates screeched encouragement. The biggest boy on the opposite side charged to cut her off. Gabriel sucked in his breath. A fall, a sprawl, blood and howls—it was a daily occurrence. If not her, then one of the others. There was no use banning the game. She was eleven. She made her own decisions. And she would only play around the corner where he couldn't see her.

eyes open. A father had to see what a father had to see. Dana spotted the boy, made a feint to the right, then stuck out her foot to trip him as she ran to the left. The boy crashed to the ground with a scream of rage and pain. Dana kicked the ball over the crack to the roar of her friends.

Gabriel relaxed, proud of his daughter. She had managed to win without getting hurt. He tensed again. But she was about to be hurt, by him, by the news he had to give her. Heavy with dread, he opened the front door and shouted at Dana to come in for her lunch.

He had set out their meal as usual in the backyard that was almost a garden. Wildflowers and tufts of grass sprouted from the broken concrete. The stone walls glared white in the sunshine. Clothes flapped on the washing line. There was a picnic table that Gabriel had built, along with the hutch that stood empty in the corner. Both he and Dana had yet to recover from the death of their rabbit, whom they refused to replace. Sea-shells and candles marked her grave under the old tree by the shed.

Dana bounded into the yard, flushed with victory. Her eyes widened at the sight of the feast her father had prepared. All her favourite things: egg salad sandwiches, dill pickles, a tub of coleslaw, slices of pale-green melon and a bowl of fresh strawberries.

"Wow! What are we celebrating, Gabe? New job? Big gig? Festival in Europe?"

"A new job, yeah," Gabriel said uneasily. "Did you wash your hands?"

"Course I did," she lied, as she tucked into the food.

3

He waited a while before broaching the subject. She chattered on about the game and how she had outwitted the brute and why they needed a new ball. Her blue eyes were bright with laughter, her face rosy. The dark curls were tangled like a bush. She was a child, but not a child. He could see the maturity slowly dawning in her features. The narrowing of the cheekbones. The firm mouth. She would be a beauty . . . like her mother. A pang from the old wound twinged inside him but he dismissed it. He had to focus on the moment. He had to tell her they were leaving.

She was almost finished with her lunch. Having divided the strawberries evenly between them, she was eating her share one by one.

"Dana, you're not going to like this, but you gotta hear me out."

She sat up instantly, eyes hard, ready for battle. Another attempt to ban her from football? Another lecture about the state of her room? New rules to increase her share of the housework? Whenever these moments arrived, she always faced him as an equal. Living together, a family of two, they had forged their relationship over the years. He had raised her to stand up for herself, sometimes to his own chagrin. She would hear him out all right, but that didn't mean she would agree or comply.

"Professor Blackburn rang this morning. He put my name in for a job at the University of Toronto. Teaching music and Irish language in the Celtic Studies program—"

"Toronto?" Dana interrupted. "Toronto, as in *Canada*?"

She saw it coming. How could she not? Though they lived in Ireland, the country of her birth, her father was Canadian. From

She was settled in school. They both had a lot of friends. And their little council house provided security against the vagaries of a musician's earnings. There was no reason for them to move.

"It's not just the job," Gabriel pointed out. "It's for you as well. Look, you need things like bras and—"

"*Dad!!!*"

"See? You can't even talk about it with me. Your aunts Dee and Yvonne will be like big sisters. They'll help you out. And your grandmother too."

"I see them every time they visit. We don't need to live near them. I don't want to move to Canada! This is my home!"

"Canada is your home as well, because it's my home. My family are there."

"Your family are here too! Great Aunt Patsy and Uncle Tommy, your first cousins, my second cousins . . . You're always saying we've got too much family! This is our home! We're Irish!"

"I was born in Canada," Gabriel insisted quietly. "And I grew up there. I'm Irish *and* Canadian. And because I am, so are you."

Gabriel started to fiddle with the gold ring in his ear. He rubbed his hand over his bald head. These were the things he always did when he was upset. He looked young and unsure of himself. He was nearly thirty but rarely acted his age. Sometimes Dana thought of him as a big kid, less practical than herself. She was proud of him and his music, he looked like a pop star, and her friends thought he was great. But sometimes she wished he were more normal, like her best friend Emer's dad who worked in an office and wore a suit. Gabriel didn't even own one.

His voice was low and wistful.

"I want to go home, Dana. I haven't been there since . . . before you were born. I know it'll be hard for you at first, but you'll love it in the end. It's a wonderful country."

The quiet way he spoke let her know it was final. She was stunned by the enormity of what he had done, what it meant. Her whole life was about to change in ways she couldn't even begin to imagine.

She was so shocked she could hardly speak, but she did manage to splutter.

"How could you do this? Without even asking me! I HATE YOU!"

Out of the garden she stormed and into the house. A few minutes later, the bedroom door slammed.

Gabriel stared at the last strawberries in the bowl. The days ahead would not be easy. He knew what to expect: temper tantrums, crying bouts and constant quarrelling. But wasn't that part of why he was going? He needed help to raise her. While he had managed to muddle through her childhood with reasonable success, the past year had been hard. She was beginning to act like a teenager, moody and defiant. There were times when he didn't know what to do. His mother was eager to see more of her grandchild and his two younger sisters were like teens themselves. When things got rough, he could call in the cavalry.

Gabriel started to clear the table. Yes, it was the best move. For both of them. Now all he had to do was convince his daughter.

CHAPTER TWO

A BREEZE BLEW THROUGH
the open windows to cool the stuffy interior of the old Triumph Herald. Air conditioning could not be expected in a vehicle built in the 1960s. The blue leather upholstery was sweaty, Dana's legs kept sticking to the seat. She didn't complain. She had grown up in that car, sleeping in the back seat on long drives through the country, picnicking on the side of the road in the rain. Once they took it on the ferry to France when Gabriel was playing in a Celtic festival in Brittany.

She threw a furious glance at her father. Was this another part of her life she would have to give up? As the first shock of his announcement wore off, she had begun to count the things she would lose: her best friend Emer and the rest of her gang at school, her neighbourhood, playing on the street, hiking in the mountains . . . In short, she was about to lose her whole life and everything that made her happy.

"You'll make new friends when you start school in September," Gabriel had suggested at breakfast that morning.

"You can't replace people you love," she spat out. "You should know that."

As soon as the words were out, she was sorry. Her father looked as if she had hit him. He opened his mouth to say something, then closed it again.

Dana was horrified. She had wanted to hurt him but not that deeply.

"Oh Gabe ... Da ... I didn't mean ..."

They had both cried into their bowls of cereal, then hugged and apologized and did their best to make up. While such scenes were rare in the past, they were becoming more frequent as Dana grew older.

"We'll go to the glen," said Gabriel. "I've got to talk to the lads about the benefit concert. Maybe you could see a tree house."

It was a peace offering, close to a bribe. He hadn't let her near the tree houses built by the eco-warriors in the Glen of the Downs. She had been begging to get inside one since the environmental protest began earlier that summer.

It was an old story befalling an old country. Ireland had grown suddenly rich and progress was marching across the land. Green fields were disappearing under housing estates. Trees were being felled to widen roads into motorways. Though the Glen of the Downs was a nature reserve protected by law, the government had approved the construction of a four-lane highway through its heart. Eco-warriors had arrived from around the world to join the protests of Irish environmentalists. They set up some living in tents, others in shelters built high in the trees.

The Triumph Herald slowed down as the Sugar Loaf Mountain loomed ahead. Mountains squeezed the road on either side. To the right, above the treeline, an old famine wall crested the ridge like a broken crown. Painted crudely on the stone in great white letters was the cry WHO CARES FOR THE GLEN?

The Glen of the Downs was a deep gorge torqued by the tidal forces of an ancient glacier. Its steep sides sheered skywards, cloaked in rich woodland. The upper slopes were dense with stately oak while ash and hazel thrived on the valley floor. A fine stand of beech grew to the west of the road, bordered by a mountain stream. As a National Nature Reserve, the glen was home to countless birds, red squirrels, badgers and fox and was the only site in Ireland for several species of insects.

Gabriel parked the Triumph beneath a cloth banner strung between two trees. NO MOTORWAY HERE. The forest rose up immediately only feet from the road. Dana was out of the car in an instant. She breathed in the smell of damp earth, old wood, wet leaves and grass. She loved this place. She and Gabriel hiked there often. When the protest began, they had joined immediately, helping with petitions, supplies and fundraising. Though many local people viewed the eco-warriors as hippies and troublemakers, there was also widespread support in the community for "the tree people."

WE DO NOT INHERIT THE EARTH FROM OUR PARENTS, WE BORROW IT FROM OUR CHILDREN.

IN WILDERNESS IS THE PRESERVATION OF THE WORLD.

WHERE TREES ARE, LIFE IS.

The banners waved from the trees like flags. Dana ran past them towards the clearing where the eco-warriors had their campfire. Here they gathered for meetings and meals, or companionship when they weren't on duty. As long as the protesters occupied the woods, the developers couldn't begin felling. Legal evictions were being pursued, but meanwhile publicity and support were growing.

After weeks of living outdoors and sleeping rough, the eco-warriors looked a bit wild, as if gone to seed. In muddy boots and soiled clothing, with straggly hair and unshaven faces, they sat around the fire on old chairs and a burst sofa. Dana thought of them as a gang of outlaws, Robin Hood and his Merry Men. Big Bob was the leader, a bear of a man with a booming voice. Mick was his right-hand man, thin and nervous, always talking on his cellphone. Billie was a young Maid Marian, an English traveller with jewellery in her ears and nose.

"How's the youngest eco-warrior in Ireland?" Big Bob said to Dana, smothering her in a hug.

She was thrilled to be part of their group, their cause. It was all very exciting.

They made room for her at the fire. A blackened pot sat in the flames, boiling water for tea. Cracked cups and mugs were passed around. Everyone smelled of burnt wood. Whenever a breeze billowed smoke from the fire, no one moved out of its path. Instead, they sat like ghosts in a fog. When Gabriel joined them, the talk turned to injunctions and legal battles.

band break up? Da giving you a hard time? Do you want me to box his ears?"

Gabriel tried to signal to Bob to let matters lie, but it was too late. Dana sensed an ally.

"He's taking us away! He's going back to Canada and he's dragging me with him!"

Big Bob looked at Gabriel with dismay.

"You're not leaving us, Gabe! When? Why?"

Billie offered Dana a chocolate biscuit while Mick passed around the milk and sugar for tea.

"I've been offered a job. The money's too good to pass up. And I think it's time. Time to go. Time to let go . . ."

His voice trailed away as he stared into the flames.

Looks passed between his friends. Gently they changed the subject to the benefit concert.

Dana saw her chance for support had vanished. Her heart sank. Would no one take her side? Was she all alone? She would not give up. She would fight the move at every turn. But she needed a plan. She heaved a deep sigh, scuffed the ground with her feet. When would she get to see a tree house? And what about another biscuit?

Billie caught her eyeing the empty packet.

"There's more in the cave. Help yourself."

That was all the encouragement Dana needed. The "cave" was a clapboard shack built under the trees, open in front and lined with shelves. Inside was a clutter of supplies and equipment used by the campers: books and maps, binoculars and compasses, a small black telescope, rain jackets, tarpaulins, sleeping bags and flashlights. Dana was rummaging through the tinned goods and groceries when a blast of wind hit the shelter. Everything rattled and shook for a moment. Nothing was upset, except for a package of biscuits which landed at her feet.

"Good one," she murmured and stooped to pick it up.

That's when she saw him, leaning against a tree outside, staring straight at her. He was a tall young man, dressed completely in black, with a broad-rimmed hat lined with holly and ivy. His features were striking, pale and handsome. His red-gold hair was tied back in a ponytail. It was the eyes that struck her the most, shining like blue stars. There was something extraordinary about him though Dana couldn't say what. She felt shy and a little in awe. Dumbly, she stepped towards him to offer the biscuits.

He smiled, shook his head.

"Follow the greenway."

His voice reminded her of Gabriel's flute.

"What?"

He reached for his hat. She thought he was saluting her, but he plucked a leaf from the brim and handed it to her. A ticket? An invitation?

"My Lady awaits you. *Follow the greenway.*"

Though he spoke quietly, it was undoubtedly a command. Dana opened her mouth to ask questions but before she could speak, he tipped his hat in farewell and walked into the woods.

"Wait a minute," she called.

Another blast of wind shook the trees. The young man was gone.

"That was weird," Dana thought to herself.

that description fitted most of Gabe's friends. Dana returned to the campfire. More tea was being brewed. More plans were being made. She groaned. They would be there all day.

"Dad, I'm bored. Can I *please* see the tree houses? Please? Please?"

"Let her go, Gabe. She's safe here," Big Bob insisted. "We're all over the place, like guardian angels."

"All right then. But don't go near the road, don't climb any trees—I'll take you up later—and shout if you need me."

"Aye, aye, captain," said Dana smartly.

She raced off before he could think up more rules.

Big Bob grinned as he watched her disappear through the trees.

"She's getting big, Gabe. Heading for womanhood."

"Don't I know it," Gabriel sighed. "It's one of the reasons I'm going home. She's been a real handful lately."

"Eleven is a tough age," Big Bob said. "Neither fish nor fowl. Half kid, half teen. I'm glad my lot are well out of it."

"She needs a mother," Gabriel said softly.

"Aye," his friend agreed sadly, gazing into the fire.

CHAPTER THREE

Dᴀɴᴀ ʜᴀᴅɴ'ᴛ ɢᴏɴᴇ ғᴀʀ when she spotted a tree house high in an old beech. The floor and walls were made of wooden pallets. A blue plastic sheet covered the roof, crackling in the wind. Ropes dangled down the tree trunk for climbing upwards.

"Anyone home?" Dana called.

No answer.

She couldn't resist the temptation. Disobeying Gabriel wasn't hard, especially when they were fighting, and Dana loved to climb trees. She tied one of the ropes round her waist and used the other to heave herself upwards. Half-climbing, half-swinging, slowly but surely she made her way to the edge of the tree house. Then she clambered on board.

Heady stuff to be so high in the treetops! Below snaked the road and the white ribbon of stream. The susurrus of speeding cars blended with the sounds of running water. All around, as far as the eye could see, wove the dark-green lace of the forest canopy. A wisp of smoke from a campfire rose through the trees. Dana grinned to herself. Gabe would have a fit if he looked up and spied her. She thumbed her nose in his direction.

There wasn't much to see inside the tree house: damp cushions scattered over a musty rug, two sleeping bags laid out, some books and papers, a few candles in jars. Shaded by leafage, the place was dark and dank and cold. When the mountain wind blew, the little house swayed along with the tree. Dana didn't stay long.

As she eased herself back down the trunk, something caught her eye. A flash of light on the slope above. Something in the woods? Someone with a mirror? She continued her descent, moving carefully to avoid a plummet. There it was again! In the greenery, a burst of gold light, as if the sun were caught in a net of branches.

When Dana reached the ground, she sensed something had changed. The forest was different. Impossibly still. Not a leaf moved, no wind sighed, nothing scrabbled in the underbrush where small creatures lived. It was as if the woods were holding its breath.

Then she heard it, high up in the air, a piper piping away. She had never heard such music, so sweet and so sad. Tears sprang to her eyes.

"Dad?"

Like Gabriel's music, it seemed to call her. Dana didn't stop to think. She scrambled up the ridge towards the sound. The way was difficult, steep and treacherous. The ground was tangled with tree roots and pocked with stones. The smell of bruised as herself. Intent on her climb, she didn't notice the road falling far behind her. The camp was now well out of earshot.

A gust of wind rolled down the mountain. Leaves swirled at Dana's feet. Startled, she saw little faces in the eddy. Narrow eyes and wide mouths. Brown crinkled skin. She blinked and they were gone. But the strange sight had stopped her headlong rush. And the music had ceased. She looked around her.

She was high in the farthest reaches of the glen, near the top of the ridge. A great oak tree stood before her. A ladder of thick ivy hung down its trunk. The ladder led upwards to a tree house so high in the branches it seemed to touch the sky. It was not at all like the other one, not roughly put together. This had a natural grace and form as if it grew from the tree itself.

Dana shivered. Her skin was tingling. She wanted to go up, but it was too high, too far. Fear and daring battled inside her. Was that a whisper in the leaves, on the wind?

Follow the greenway.

She grasped the ladder. Her foot settled on the lowest rung. Then she hurried upwards before she could change her mind. The lower branches of the tree brushed against her as she pushed through to climb higher. Up and up again. She had to stop looking down as it made her dizzy. At last she reached the crown of the oak to find the loveliest tree house imaginable.

Slender branches were meshed together to form a dome. The walls were woven with marigolds, bluebells and pink and white foxglove. The windows were round like big eyes and the door was an archway. Dana lowered her head to step inside. The interior was green with dappled light. The scent of wildflowers perfumed the air. The moss-covered floor was speckled with blossoms of whitethorn strewn about like confetti. It was a magical place, but no more magical than the person who awaited her.

Seated on the floor at a low wooden table was a young woman of startling beauty. Her golden skin shimmered faintly. Her hair was as fair as the blossoms that wreathed her head. She wore a gown of green silk, a yellow cloak, and daisy chains for jewellery around her neck. On the table before her a small feast was laid out: bowls of crisp nuts and fat berries, plates of oaten cakes dripping with honey, glass goblets brimming with a dark purple wine.

A hippie girl, Dana thought, perhaps an English traveller like Billie? But the label didn't fit. There was something . . . queenly . . . about her. An eccentric aristocrat perhaps? Dana's father knew all kinds of odd sods and bods.

Dana spluttered out apologies for barging in. The Lady smiled.

"*Fáilte romhat,*" she said, inviting Dana to sit with a wave of her hand. "I welcome thee to my forest fane."

Her voice was musical, silvery. Not a hippie, Dana decided, but both her English and her Irish sounded strange. Definitely eccentric. Breathless with a huge and nameless excitement, Dana sat down.

"Eat and drink with me," said the Lady.

Never had a hazelnut tasted so nutty! Never had a blackberry burst on the tongue with such sweet tartness! As for the little honeyed cakes, they were like sunlight dusted with sugar.

Dana gulped down another cake before answering.

"My dad and I have been involved right from the start. He's organizing a concert. He's at the campfire right now with—"

The Lady shook her head gently.

"You alone, dear heart. The High King needs you to bear a message."

"*High King*? Since when did we have a king? What are you—"

The Lady's gaze was steady. Her eyes gleamed like blue stars.

"Do you not know who we are?" she asked.

Dana was bewildered. Something was pressing inside her. She found it difficult to breathe.

"Aren't you . . . one of . . . the tree people?"

The Lady nodded gravely.

"That is one of our names. I am of the Tree People."

Dana shivered. She heard the capital letters and sensed the huge significance that lurked behind them. But she couldn't begin to understand, and the Lady was saying more confusing things.

"I am of the Tree People behind the tree people. We inspire their work. The destruction of the forest is the beginning of the end of our world."

Dana didn't know what to think or how to react. This was beyond eccentric. Was the girl on drugs? Dana was growing more nervous by the minute. This was too weird, even scary. She opened her mouth to yell for her father but found herself yawning instead. She was spellbound. *Fairy struck*. Her eyelids were heavy, she wanted to sleep.

The Lady saw what was happening and panicked.

"Do not succumb, Dana! Thou art a child and shouldst be of stronger mind than older mortals. Come out of your swoon! We have need of thee!"

It was too much to ask, even of a child, especially a child of the modern world. As Dana's eyes closed to shut out the impossible, she drifted into the safe harbours of sleep.

The Lady buried her face in her hands.

"I cannot reach her! Lost to me are human ways and speech. I cannot gain her trust nor secure her assurances. I have failed the Summer Land!"

The tears and laments didn't wake Dana but the sudden transformation that followed did.

"Omigod! You're only a kid! How could I possibly send you on a dangerous mission?"

Dana's eyes sprang open. The North American accent was like a cold splash of water. What was going on? She rubbed her eyes. Everything was different. Though the young woman was still pretty, she had lost her *glamour*. The golden sheen was gone from her skin and the startling blue eyes were now hazel-green. The blonde hair was far less shiny and a tangled mess. No longer "the Lady," she looked like a teenager and a bit of a hippie.

Dana was stunned.

"Who are you?"

"My name's Honor."

The voice was the biggest shock. The silvery tone was gone, replaced with a clearly Canadian accent.

"You're not even Irish!"

Honor herself looked surprised and confused.

new to the whole thing. This has never happened before." She touched her hair with dismay. "Maybe I was so upset at not getting through to you, that I returned to my old self. You see we . . . they . . . You're really needed, Dana. Big time. We've got to get a message to the *tánaiste*. You're the only way we can reach him."

"I don't know what you're talking about," Dana said. "What *tánaiste*? Do you mean in the government?"

"No, no, not your *tánaiste*. Our *tánaiste*. The second-in-command to the High King. After a long search through all kinds of oracles—clouds, the flight of birds, the flame of a thousand lamps and so on—we finally got a name. *Lugh of the Mountain, Lugh of the Wood.* The King of Wicklow. We tried to send him messengers but they were turned back at the border—"

"None of this makes sense!" Dana interrupted. She was fighting hard not to be frightened but it was all very weird. "Look, I'm eleven years old. How could I possibly help you? And even if I could, why should I? You're a complete stranger to me!"

Honor frowned, obviously struggling with her thoughts. Dana wondered again if she might be on drugs. But she seemed quite nice, if rather scatterbrained. Despite the odd behaviour, Dana felt she could like her.

"Okay, I'll be honest here," Honor said at last, speaking slowly. "I seem to have forgotten a lot of things. I guess because I've reverted . . . Anyway, there's a good reason why King Lugh will listen to you and no one else, but I can't remember what it is. Also, you can travel through his land because you're not bound by our laws. That answers why we need you. Kind of. As for your other question—why should you help us?"

Honor leaned forward. Her eyes sparkled with mischief. She burst into a grin so wide that Dana couldn't help but smile back.

"This I *do* know," she said, in a conspiratorial tone, "though I'm not sure if I'm supposed to tell you. If you do something for them . . . I mean us . . . then, in return, we owe something to you."

At last she was saying things Dana could grasp.

"What kind of something?"

Honor looked around quickly, then shrugged and giggled.

"Your heart's desire. Your wish come true."

CHAPTER FOUR

She was lost in an
abysmal place of flying forms and dark spaces. There was no sound, no
light, no warmth. She was searching for something. In the distance there
was movement. She drew near to what looked like a mountain. On the
peak was the dim shape of a house. The door opened and a child's
pram, painted black, rolled out. Over the edge of the cliff it tipped, then
it sped crazily down the hillside. A woman stood watching. Had she let
it go? Had she pushed it? Now the pram was a stone rolling onwards.
Now the woman was a tree, twisted and alone.

"MAMA!"

Dana was screaming. As always when she woke, she
changed her cry even as Gabriel rushed into the room.

"DAD! DAD!"

"I'm here, sweetheart. It's all right. I'm here."

He held her tightly till she calmed down. She often had
nightmares, especially when she was upset. Gabriel cringed

with guilt. He was certain this had to do with the news about Canada.

Dana was just as certain it didn't.

"I shouldn't have touched the feast," she murmured.

"What feast?" Gabriel asked gently to humour her.

"At the glen."

It was just a suspicion. Dana had grown up on the tales that warned against taking food or drink from "the Good People."

"The cups were pretty dirty," Gabriel agreed. "But my mother always said, 'you have to eat a peck of dirt before you die.'"

"Yuk," said Dana.

Fully awake now, she didn't explain her words. She hadn't told Gabriel about the Lady in the woods. Best to change the subject.

"How about a midnight snack?"

They padded down the stairs in their pyjamas. It was three o'clock in the morning, the usual time for Dana's nightmares. They were always the same. The pram and the woman. The stone and the tree. Unless she had school the next day, the two usually headed down to the kitchen for a chat and a treat.

The house was small and narrow. Each had their own bedroom upstairs while below were the living and dining rooms, bathroom and kitchen. The living room was Gabriel's work space with his equipment, instruments, desk and computer. The sofa and television went in the dining room along with the bookshelves, table and chairs. They usually ate in the kitchen on stools against the counter, except in good weather when they ate outdoors.

the toaster and set out the dishes.

"It's been a while since you had a bad dream, eh?" Gabriel ventured.

"Hmmm," said Dana.

The gas flame flickered blue and orange beneath the pot. She tested the temperature of the milk with a tentative finger. How could she possibly tell him what had happened in the forest? The pact she had made with Honor? The wish she could earn? It was all too wild and unbelievable. She hardly believed it herself.

Gabriel regarded his daughter as she stood at the stove, peering into the pot. She looked so vulnerable, all arms and legs in her baggy pyjamas, dark hair rumpled from sleep. He wanted to make things easier for her.

"Look, Dana. How about we agree to try it, just for a year or maybe two? If you're really miserable, if it doesn't work out, we'll come back. I swear."

She met his reassuring look with the straight honest gaze of a child.

"If we move to Canada, Gabe, how will she find us?"

He was stunned. He almost cried. Why hadn't he guessed? How could he not have known? He stuttered through his words.

"Dana . . . sweetheart . . . we've been through this before . . . We both have to accept . . . I thought you had . . . It's been over seven years . . . *Your mother's not coming back.*"

Her features hardened.

"You don't know that for sure. And . . . things change. You never know what can happen."

He began to flounder, thinking wildly. This was a matter they had resolved long ago. Or so he believed. Was the shock of the move setting her back? He decided to take it a step at a time, the way he used to when she was small and still full of questions.

"You know the story, kiddo, but I don't mind telling you again, and I'll continue to tell you as long as you need it.

"Your mother and I were madly in love but we were very young. Kids really, both in our teens. Too young to marry. We rented an old cottage above the Glen of the Downs. She wouldn't live in the town. She was a country girl. You were born a year later. We were poor but happy. Your mother grew vegetables in the garden, made her own bread and just about everything else we ate. Okay, I'll admit it, we were hippies. I played in pubs, taught students, even busked on the streets. We got by. It wasn't hard, believe me, we were really happy. And you were a great baby, always laughing."

His face shone as he remembered. Then he lowered his voice, his features darkened.

"It was like a lightning bolt out of the blue. That's the only way I can describe it. I left a happy home that morning and when I came back for lunch, everything had changed. Changed utterly."

Dana put her hand on her father's shoulder. He didn't cry, all his tears had been shed years ago, but his body was clenched like a fist.

"I found you in the house alone, crying your heart out. She was gone. Without warning or explanation. Not even a note. The police suspected suicide, but when they searched the lakes and rivers, there was no sign of her. In the end, they called her a runaway and closed the case."

seep through the sky to light up the backyard. The wild roses trailing over the shed glowed red in the dimness.

"And that's when we moved here," Dana finished for him. "To Wolfe Tone Square in the town of Bray. To a little neighbourhood where I found friends and you found a new life. And though we missed her terribly at first, we both slowly got over it and lived happily ever after."

Gabriel smiled at his daughter. She *was* growing up.

Dana smiled back. In truth, she had stopped thinking about her mother a long time ago. Like most children faced with intolerable tragedy, she had put it away in the back of her mind and got on with her life.

But the meeting with the Lady in the woods had changed all that. No sooner had Honor mentioned the wish than Dana thought of her mother. The flicker of hope was like a candle in the dark. She could now think about the unthinkable.

"Why can't I remember her, Gabe? How come I have no memories? I close my eyes, I try to find one, and I can't."

"You were only three. But you know what she looked like from the photo album."

"It's not the same! I mean a picture in my head, of *her* looking at *me*. I can do it with you, even from way back then. I shut my eyes and there you are, looking at me."

Dana closed her eyes. Her face lit up. Gabriel's heart gladdened. She obviously saw his love for her. When she opened her eyes again, her look was fierce.

"When I try to do that for mum, nothing comes. Nothing's there. Gabe—did she not love me? Is that why she left?"

For the second time that night he was struck speechless. He jumped up to grasp hold of her.

"You mustn't think that! Jesus, Dana, we went over this when you were little. All kids blame themselves when their parents split up, even if one dies. I've told you again and again, it's not your fault! It had nothing to do with you. How could it? You were three years old! An innocent baby! Look, maybe I was fooling myself and I was doing it all wrong, but the way I remember it, the three of us were happy. Really happy. I can tell you this for certain—she loved me and she loved you."

"Then why did she go?"

They had arrived at the point Gabriel always reached whenever he went on this journey. A dark place of defeat and unknowing. A dead end.

His sigh was low and sad.

"Like I said, we were very young, just kids. Maybe it was too much for her. I don't know. The truth is, I can't answer that question, though I never stop trying. I don't know why she left. I don't think we'll ever know."

CHAPTER FIVE

Dana was beginning to
panic. More than a week had passed since her adventure in
the glen, since she had made her pact with the Lady in the
woods. In return for a wish, Dana had agreed to bear a message to King Lugh of Wicklow. Before they parted, Honor
promised to send for her soon, but time was running out. The
tickets to Canada were booked for September, only one
month away.

Dana was beginning to fear she had imagined the whole
thing. A desperate dream of a last-minute reprieve. Then again,
whenever she believed it was real, she was overcome with a different kind of fear. These were obviously matters beyond the
ordinary. Honor had even spoken of danger. Could Dana do
this? She wished her best friend, Emer, weren't away on holidays. There was no one she could talk to. Who would believe
her? She had decided in the end she couldn't tell Gabriel. Aside

from the fact he would think it was crazy, he would never let her go off on her own!

Things were also tense at home. Since Gabriel travelled on a Canadian passport, he had to prove his right to take Dana from her homeland. Officially, the mother's consent was required. The issue of her disappearance was raised once more. Statements were requested from the police. Notices had to be posted giving her the chance to come forward to claim her child. It was harrowing for Gabriel.

Though he didn't involve Dana, she could see the strain in his eyes and the droop of his shoulders. She wanted to give him a hard time about Canada, but she found she couldn't. He looked too miserable.

"Come on, Gabe, let's go out for dinner," she suggested that day. "We haven't celebrated your new job."

She had to look away quickly. She could always tell when he wanted to cry.

The Hanuman House was their favourite place in Bray not only because it served Indian food but because they knew its owners, Aradhana and Suresh. Two flights of stairs led upwards to a spacious dining room overlooking the river. The walls of the restaurant were beautifully painted with scenes from the Hindu epic, the *Ramayana*.

Dana loved the pictures and the story, it was all so romantic. How the hero Rama saved his wife, Sita, who was stolen by the evil demon Ravanna. The paintings seemed to come alive especially after dusk when candles were lit at the tables. Shadows would dance on the walls as the music of tambours and sitars wept softly through the room.

humorous older brother. Slender and graceful, with great dark eyes, she was as lovely as the portraits of Sita. Her silken sari swished as she walked. Jasmine trailed through her long black braid. This was how she dressed for work. Whenever they met her on the streets of Bray, she wore jeans and a T-shirt and her hair in a ponytail.

Dana and her father were also dressed up. Gabriel wore white trousers and a blue silk shirt. Both his head and his gold earring shone in the candlelight. Dana had on a long denim skirt with a silver blouse and high platform shoes.

"How is my Irish Barbie this evening?" Aradhana said as she led them to their table.

Dana would have hated to be called this by anyone else, but Aradhana was so kind and gracious that she didn't mind. Dana wasn't the only one the young woman charmed. Gabriel always acted oddly when she was around. Once Dana teased him to ask for a date, but he had answered seriously.

"My girlfriends never last, you know that. Aradhana's special. I wouldn't want to ruin our friendship."

Dana watched wryly as her father puzzled over the menu to keep Aradhana beside him. He enquired about various dishes and sought out her advice, though he knew quite well they would have what they always had—vegetable balti, basmati rice, peshwari bread stuffed with nuts and raisins, and two frothing glasses of mango lassi.

While Gabriel dragged out the process as long as he could, Dana wandered over to her favourite scene, the reunion of Rama and Sita. As she gazed at the picture of the two lovers entwined, a little old lady hobbled up beside her. Leaning on a knobbled stick of whitethorn, she wore a long red skirt and a dark-green shawl. Wisps of smoky grey hair framed the narrow face sprinkled with whiskers. The eyes were like two beads of black glass.

"*Is breá an tráthnóna é*," she said to Dana. "A fine evening indeed."

"*'Sea*," agreed Dana, politely. "*Conas tá tú, a mháthair?*"

The old woman grasped Dana's hands.

"You must come, my pet. You must come to the mountains."

Then, before Dana could react, she had scurried away with surprising speed, out of the restaurant.

Dana returned to her seat, flushed with excitement. This was the sign she had been waiting for.

"Gabe," she declared, "I need to go into the mountains. You've got to take me."

"Since I have nothing else to do," he pointed out.

She knew that face. It wasn't open to negotiation. But by the time Aradhana had brought their dinner, Dana had a plan.

"When's your next day off?" she asked the young woman.

"Dana—" Gabriel started, but she was too quick for him.

"Didn't you say you've never been to Powerscourt?"

Aradhana nodded. "There are many places I have still to visit. A year is not enough to set up a business. No time for holidays."

"We should take her on a picnic, Gabe! To the waterfall. It would be a break from the packing and a little farewell party too."

"Packing? Farewell?" Aradhana's voice quavered. She avoided looking at Gabriel. "Are you leaving us, my Irish Barbie?"

"Not that I want to," Dana said, glad of the unexpected support. "Gabe's dragging me to Canada."

Aradhana's face brightened.

"Ah, Canada. It is a wonderful place. Many Indian people live there. I have cousins in Toronto."

"That's where we're going!" Gabriel cried.

They were like two people rescued from drowning. Dana was nonplussed. She couldn't remember her father looking at any of his girlfriends this way.

"Are you emigrating so?" Aradhana asked softly.

"Actually, I'm going home. My parents are Irish but I was born in Canada and grew up there. I have two homes."

"You are like me, then. I have two homes also."

Dana heard the wistful echo in her voice. It was the same tone she had used when she spoke of the many Indians in Canada. There were few in Ireland. Was she homesick? Was she lonely? Who else did she have besides her brother and the staff? The more Dana thought of Aradhana, the more she liked her, though she didn't really want to. Gabe already liked her enough for the two of them. And now the plan was succeeding all too well, with her father enthusing about the picnic despite the work he had to do. As soon as Aradhana named her day off, the date was set.

It was later, when they were eating dessert, that Dana spotted the young couple at the take-away counter. At first glance they looked like any teenaged pair, in tight jeans and skimpy tops, arms wrapped around each other. Honor's blonde hair fell over her shoulders. Her boyfriend sported a red-gold ponytail. Dana recognized him from the campfire. One of the tree people? Or one of the Tree People?

"Hey, look at the fairies!" Gabriel exclaimed.

"What?" gasped Dana.

He was pointing at the wall behind her. She spun around. It was one of the early scenes from the *Ramayana*, before Sita was kidnapped, when she and Rama lived in the forest. There to the left, amidst the trees, were figures Dana had never noticed before. Half-hidden in the leafy shadows, they were shadowy themselves, dark-eyed and dark-skinned, with faint shapes at their shoulders. The wisp of wings.

"I've never seen them before!"

Aradhana came over when Gabriel called her.

"We have fairies in India," she told him. "We call them *devas*. The artist must have known. I can't remember her name. I think she lives in the mountains."

"I bet she does," Dana muttered.

She looked around. Honor and her boyfriend were gone.

CHAPTER SIX

POWERSCOURT WAS A GREAT country estate refurbished by a viscount in the late nineteenth century. The stone mansion was as grand as a palace set in the midst of Italianate gardens, an ornamental lake and sculptured fountains. Two miles from the manor house, the demesne ran wild into a rocky valley with a deer park and woods. Here fell the highest waterfall in Ireland, streaming like silver down three hundred feet of dark rock. The site was open to the public, with a parking lot, picnic area and nature trail.

"It's beautiful here," said Aradhana, as she spread their blanket on the ground near the falls. "Listen to the birds!"

Gabriel unpacked the basket of crusty salad rolls, various cheeses from the deli, pickles and olives, fruit and chocolates. There was a bottle of white wine for the adults and cola for Dana. Aradhana had brought her own contribution to the picnic, much to the delight of the other two—vegetable samosas, pakoras and crispy pappadams with raita.

"You can hear the nightjar at dusk on a summer evening," Gabriel told her.

"Really? What does it sound like?"

"Haven't a clue," he admitted. "I read it in the brochure at the gate."

They laughed.

They were doing a lot of laughing, Dana noted. She was beginning to have mixed feelings about their friendship. She liked Aradhana, but she had other hopes for her father.

"Let's paddle in the waterfall!" she suggested, catching Aradhana's hand. "Dad can fix lunch."

"Yes, go ahead and have fun without me," said Gabriel. "I'll just work away here, all by myself."

It was a hot summer's day. They took off their sandals and plunged into the pool at the foot of the waterfall. The spray cooled their faces. Dana wore shorts and a cotton T-shirt. Her dark curls fell loose on her shoulders. Aradhana had rolled her trousers up to the knee. She was dressed in pale colours, beige and cream. Her black hair gleamed in the sunlight.

Dana picked wood sorrel from a cleft in the wet rock and offered it to Aradhana.

"Gabe calls it 'chip chop cherry.' Tastes like cherry-flavoured chewing gum."

Aradhana chewed it thoughtfully. "Tart but tasty. I will try it in a salad, perhaps even a sauce." She smiled at Dana. "I shall miss my Irish Barbie."

They circled each other in the sunlit water.

"I don't want to go. It's not fair that adults get to make the decisions."

"It is unfair," Aradhana agreed. "But you will be an adult yourself one day and then you will be in charge of your life."

"That seems a long way away," Dana sighed.

She sat down on the rocks and kicked her feet in the water.

"We are alike, you know," Aradhana said, sitting down beside her. "I was reared by my father also. There was just Suresh and me. Our mother died when we were very young and our father never remarried. His heart was broken and could not mend to love another."

"That's sad," said Dana, but she was uneasy.

Gabriel's heart had broken too and never mended. Dana wanted him to be happy, but not now, not yet. Aradhana was wonderful and if there was no hope at all . . . no hope of finding her mother . . . then . . . but there was hope now and Dana would do anything to keep it alive. If she earned her wish, she could find her mother and reunite her parents. Then they would all stay in Ireland and live happily ever after.

"Do you believe in fairies?"

Dana's question was sudden and earnest.

Aradhana smiled, but without condescension.

"This question of belief is difficult for people in the West, yes? It is easy if you are born a Hindu. You grow up knowing many gods and goddesses, many kinds of spirits and beings."

"Irish people believe in a lot too," Dana pointed out. "God and the Mother of God and angels and saints. Dad says a lot of people still believe in fairies."

"And you?"

Dana looked uncertain. "Well, weird things can happen but it seems kind of ... childish ... like still believing in Santa Claus."

Aradhana gazed up at the great falls that tumbled towards them.

"I would not want to live in a world without gods or fairies. I am happy to think that life is full of mystery."

Gabriel shouted over to them.

"Hey you two mermaids! Come and join a poor mortal who's starving to death!"

Throughout the picnic, Dana kept looking around. She was expecting something, though she didn't know what. She had come to the mountains, as directed. Just over the ridge, beyond the falls, was the Wicklow Way, a nature trail that led to the heart of the hills.

They were finishing their meal when it happened. Only Dana saw the mist that snaked through the trees like smoke. Only Dana heard the whispers on the wind.

Follow the greenway.

The mist rolled in fast, filling the valley like a pea-souper fog. Dana glanced at Gabriel and Aradhana to see if they noticed. They were frozen in their places! Everything had stopped. No water fell. No birds sang. The world was still, in a haze of silver.

The whispers around Dana grew insistent. Invisible hands began to tug at her clothes. She understood. It was time to go.

She balked. After all the high hopes and dreams, wishful thinking and fantasies, she now faced the reality. The price to be paid, the sacrifice to be made. She would have to leave Gabriel. Without warning or explanation, without knowing for how long, she would have to leave him even as her mother had left him. Her heart almost stopped at the thought of his pain.

Dana's resolve faltered. She could hardly bear it. What should she do? The whispers around her were frantic. She was being poked and pinched and pushed and pulled.

Follow the greenway.

High on the ridge, above the waterfall, Honor waved urgently.

Dana turned to her father. Frozen in mid-act, he was passing a glass of wine to Aradhana. With a pang she saw the look in his eyes. In real time, he hid it, blinking shyly. Caught in the stillness, it shone like a beacon. His love for the woman. Dana didn't want to turn to their friend. She was afraid for Gabriel, who might be spurned; afraid for herself, not wanting the complication; afraid for her mother, who might be replaced forever. Dana took a deep breath and looked. Like the sun reflected on the surface of a lake, the same love shone there in Aradhana's eyes.

Dana grabbed her rucksack. It was already packed for a journey: jeans and sweater, socks and running shoes, her waterproof jacket, a flashlight and batteries. Now she shovelled in food, the big bottle of cola and handfuls of chocolates. Her mind was made up. She had to go. She had to find her mother before it was too late. Before things progressed. Before people got hurt.

She kissed her father's cheek and hugged his still body. *I love you, Da.* She embraced Aradhana and whispered in her ear. *Look after him.*

Then she hurried away, climbing upwards. Towards the greenway.

Chapter Seven

Dana climbed slowly up the ridge. She could barely see through the mist that scarved the valley. Cold fingers continued to prod her. Slowly the sounds of the vale returned, the chatter of birds and the rush of the waterfall.

She did not look back. Not even when Gabriel and Aradhana called out. She could hear the panic in their voices. Heard especially the pain in her father's.

"Dana? Dana! Where are you?"

The invisible hands clutched her tightly, as if afraid that human voices could yet draw her back. She was near the top. A slender arm reached down and hauled her onto the summit. There stood Honor in shorts and a halter top, peaked cap and sunglasses. Her hair was tied back in a blonde braid. She grinned at Dana.

"Are you coming with me?" Dana asked, happy at the thought.

Honor's tone was regretful.

"I can't. None of us can go into the mountains without King Lugh's permission. I'm here for another reason, Dana. I've come to warn you. I don't think you should go. It will be dangerous. You're too young."

"But you're the one—!"

"I know and when I'm . . . like them . . . I don't see the problem. That's the way they are. They'll use mortals for their own ends without thinking twice about it. But I still have human feelings at times."

"Is that why you keep changing?" Dana was intrigued. "Are you a new . . . fairy?" She was uneasy with the word though it seemed silly to be shy of it. After all, Honor spoke of humans as if they were aliens.

The other girl laughed. For a moment the air around them brightened.

"Yes, I am a young fairy. And they are all so very very old. Older than the moon. Like stars gone to seed and run wild in the world." She sighed. "But they don't have human thoughts or feelings. They put their own good over everyone else's. I've told the High King this is wrong. You're just a kid. There must be others who could do the job."

Dana was terrified by Honor's words and more so by her tone. Why did people always believe they knew what was best for you? Her voice rose as she argued.

"You can't do this! You promised! Look, you don't know me. I need that wish. It's the most important thing in the world to me. It's my chance to find my mother and stay in Ireland. I'll do anything to get it! I can do this. I know it!"

"The High King says you're the one . . ." Honor spoke slowly, as if to convince herself. "He says mortals always underestimate their children."

"He's right!" exclaimed Dana. "We're so much smarter than adults think we are. I've been doing things for myself since I was little. I'm strong. I can take care of myself. I can do anything any teenager can do. You've got to let me do this. You've got to let me go."

Even when Honor finally consented, she didn't look happy. Linking arms with Dana, she led her through the forest that ranged from Powerscourt to the edge of the Wicklow Mountains.

"I'm afraid for you, Dana. This is not a simple mission. The shadow is rising against us. It will try to stop you. I have told my people to keep watch for you but I can't guarantee your safety."

As they walked together, Dana noticed strange things at the edge of her vision. The trees seemed to bow towards them. When they passed a clump of wild rose, a flurry of petals showered their path. Small birds kept swooping above their heads in arabesques of flight. At first, Honor seemed unaware, but then Dana caught her waving her hand graciously. In that moment she was the Lady.

"We don't know why King Lugh will not answer our call. And the mountain fairies belong first to him. They are wild, many are solitaries. Some will help, but others will hinder you."

"I'll do my best to succeed in my mission," Dana said firmly. "You want me to take a message to the *tánaiste*? Where can I find him and what do I say?"

"Lugh of the Mountain, Lugh of the Wood dwells in his palace beneath Lugnaquillia—"

"The highest mountain in Wicklow!" said Dana. "I know it! I've seen it. My dad and I hike a lot, but I haven't climbed Lug yet. I've always wanted to."

Honor looked pleased.

"Perhaps the High King is right and this won't be too hard for you. Here is the message: *A shadow is crossing the land. The Enemy rises. Where is the light to bridge the darkness?*"

Dana was baffled.

"What does it mean?"

"The *tánaiste* will understand. When King Lugh hears the message, he will know what to do."

They had reached the edge of the forest. Beyond stretched the Wicklow Mountains as far as the eye could see.

Honor was looking anxious again.

"Do you have a jacket? Put it on and keep your ears covered. It's windy in the hills. Have you got stuff to eat and drink in your knapsack? I can't go beyond this point. We've reached the borders of the King of Wicklow. Now remember, travel always westwards. Towards the setting sun."

"I'll be okay," Dana assured her. "You'll see. You won't be sorry."

They hugged farewell. Reluctantly, Honor turned to leave, then she stopped. Her sudden smile was a burst of sunshine.

"I just remembered! Sorry, I'm such a dope being betwixt and between. I can give you a gift! It's tradition. Something magical to help you on your quest."

She clapped her hands in the air. In her palm appeared a

tiny gold case with a jewelled clasp. Inside was a red pomade that smelled of apples.

"Close your eyes," she told Dana.

As she dabbed the sweet balm onto each eyelid, she explained its use.

"This will let you see what mortals cannot see unless we allow them. Your eyes will pierce the veil that cloaks our land from yours. You will know that Faerie is all around you. Those whom you'll see will assume you are blind. This will give you time to judge who is friend or foe."

Dana was overwhelmed. Not only by the gift, but by the thought of the great adventure that lay ahead.

"Thank you," she said breathlessly. "I won't let you down."

Honor raised her hand. She stood as the Lady, wreathed in white flowers.

"My blessings upon you," she said in her silvery voice. "May you be of good courage as you follow the greenway."

Dana stepped from the shadow of the forest onto the trail that led into the mountains. Behind her, the wind whispered in the leaves of the trees.

Blessings from the Green Lady, Our Lady of the Woods. Blessings go with you from the High Queen of Faerie.

CHAPTER EIGHT

DANA FOLLOWED THE worn track into the mountains. Even as she walked the Wicklow Way, an official county hiker's trail, she was aware that she also trod a secret road in the Kingdom of Faerie. Around her rolled green hills and brown mountains, fading in the distance to hues of blue. In the north shone the stony peak of Djouce Mountain. Lugnaquillia, her destination, lay in the west.

Despite her brave words to Honor, Dana felt anxious and lonely. She was too young to have ever travelled on her own. She usually hiked with Gabriel. That he would normally be walking beside her, pointing out plants or singing songs, made her miss him all the more. She couldn't bear to think how he was taking her disappearance. How he must be suffering. She quickened her pace. Wasn't she doing this for him as well? She would find his wife. That would make it all worthwhile.

Dana hadn't gone far when she spotted a vague shape on the road ahead. Drawing near, she recognized who was sitting on the broken wall—the old woman from the Hanuman House in Bray. Dana hurried to meet her.

"I've come. Just as you said! Are you here to help me?"

The eyes were the same, dark and merry, but she seemed to have grown more whiskers on her face. She cocked her head sideways and smiled.

"Do you hear it, *mo stór? Éist nóiméad.*"

Dana listened a moment as she was directed. She had grown used to the wind hawing through the hills, but now she heard, as well, a low booming note.

"How I have longed to hear that sound," the old woman said. "The song of the bittern. She was driven from the bogs by drainage and hunters, but she is returning. Not all that is gone is gone forever."

Dana felt reassured by her words, though she wasn't sure what they meant.

"*Go raibh míle maith agat,*" she thanked her.

The old lady's face crinkled with laughter.

"You are a sweetling child. I will gladly guide you on your way. Run up this hill as fast as you can, with a heart as wild as the hearts of birds. A lovely surprise awaits you at the top. Hurry now and you will have hind's feet in high places."

"Thank you!" Dana called behind her as she started to run. "Thanks again!"

She raced up the hill as only a child can run, a child with long legs who loves to run. Free as the wind. Wild as the birds. She ran without thinking, filled with excitement and the irresistible promise of a surprise ahead. Panting, she reached the hilltop and gasped with delight.

They stiffened at her arrival, heads up, ears pricked, doe eyes staring, antlers high: a herd of wild deer.

They were a little shy but they didn't bolt. One ventured forward to nuzzle her hand and the others quickly followed. Soon she was surrounded. Soft flanks pressed against her. She sensed they were about to run. They nudged her gently.

"I don't know if I can," she whispered.

They breathed on her, warm green grassy breath. *Follow the greenway.* They breathed their nature into her. She felt a tingling in her legs. Weren't her limbs as long and graceful as a deer's? Deep inside she knew the truth. She could run as they ran.

O the joy of running with the deer! *Hind's feet in high places.* Sleek hides rippling beside her. Rising and falling like the waves of the sea. The drumming and thrumming of hooves on the earth. They ran with one mind as if of one body. At the heart of the herd, she too ran wildly. Her humanity shed like clothes in the wind. Her skin was a pelt. Antlers jutted from her brow. Her heart beat with the wild heart of the herd. She ran faster, farther, than she had ever run before.

How long they ran, Dana had no idea. The landscape blurred with the speed of their passing. They would race downhill in a blind descent, kicking up stones and soil behind them, then splash through a stream to charge upwards once more.

On the mountain of Luggala overlooking Knockna-cloghoge, they finally drew to a halt. Below in the east lay the still waters of Lough Tay. When she saw how far the herd had brought her, Dana was grateful. They butted her gently to say farewell, then raced back down the hillside.

The wind was cold on the exposed summit. Dana changed into her jeans and sweater, socks and running shoes. The afternoon was fading. She tried not to think of where she would spend the night. She wasn't worried, not yet. The summer days were long and bright. But she was already missing the company of the deer. She decided she deserved a break and sat down on a flat rock to have a picnic.

Dana was rummaging in her knapsack for something to eat when she saw them. Two feet protruding from under the rock! She jumped up with a scream.

"Are you all right?" she cried. "Have you been hurt? Can you breathe?"

A voice croaked from beneath the stone. Frantically Dana pushed against it, shouting for help in the hope some hiker might hear. The person underneath was shouting too and when the stone rolled over, he roared at Dana.

"Whist and hold your tongue, girl! You're burstin' me head!"

Speechless, Dana stared at the little man before her. He was as brown and wrinkled as an old leaf. His hair and beard had grown to his feet and were tangled around him like a nest. His clothes were brown paper tied with twine, calling to mind an abandoned parcel.

"What in the name of all that's holly and ivy are you kickin' up such a racket for?!" he demanded.

"I thought . . ." Dana stopped. Of course he hadn't been

crushed under the stone. He obviously lived there. She fought back a fit of giggles. He was really quite funny-looking.

"Are you a fairy?" she asked.

"Do I look like one?" he said testily.

"I'm sorry," she hurried to explain, "but I've only met a few. Honor told me—"

His face softened as soon as he heard the name and he raised his hand.

"No need to speak further. I've got ye now. You're the Lady's messenger. She told us to watch out for ye. Is that why you're able to see me when none of your kind do? They're always passin' this way with their big sore feet and bags of food and drink. They all sit down on Yallery Brown's bed—the Stranger's Rock they call it—and not a one of them offers me a bite to eat. You'd think I didn't have a mouth on me."

He eyed her knapsack with hope.

"I was just about to have a snack, you're welcome to share it," Dana offered. "I hate eating by myself."

They settled the big rock back in its place and spread out the food on top of it. Dana had brought a chunk of cheese, a left-over salad roll, four samosas, some pickles, apples and chocolates. Yallery Brown eyed the samosas suspiciously. He picked one up, sniffed it, looked suddenly pleased, then held it in both hands and nibbled it daintily. Dana had to fight back the giggles again. He ate the same way as her pet hamsters. She herself wolfed down the salad roll with some cheese and pickles. She was starving after her run with the deer. Munching away, they stretched their legs comfortably. Dana noticed Yallery had two left feet.

"Will ye tell me a story?" he asked. "I love human tales."

"I'm not sure what you mean. I mostly know fairy tales."

"Ah sure, they're old hat. I've heard them all. But you must know your own story?" he insisted. "Tell me that."

Dana shrugged.

"There's not much to tell really." She felt put on the spot. She wasn't good at English or composition at school. "My name's Dana Faolan. I belong to the Faolans of Wicklow, that's my dad's family. His mum, my grandmother, is a Gowan from Wexford. I don't know anything about my own mum or her family . . . I guess I've only got half a story," she concluded glumly.

Yallery Brown patted her hand.

"You are still inside your story, *a chara*. There is much more to happen. But someday, Dana Faolan, you will tell your tale and it will be one of the finest ever told."

Dana blushed at his claim and gave him a chocolate.

"You've an open hand and a generous heart," he said. "For that ye'll always be rewarded in Faerie."

Brushing the last crumbs of samosa out of his beard, Yallery searched through his pockets. He found a dandelion with its puffball intact.

"Pack up your bag! Be quick, be nimble!"

Dana hurried to gather up her things even as he blew the thistledown in her direction.

"Fare you well on your journey, little messenger. *Follow the greenway.*"

Before she could say goodbye or thank you, Yallery Brown and the mountain rushed away from her.

He had blown her farther up and further in, Dana saw that immediately. If ever there was a place for fairies, this was it. A secret and forgotten region. A stony landscape of sheer cliff and rock. There was no sign that humans had ever come here, but wherever she looked, she saw the native dwellers.

A raven landed nearby with a flap of dark wings. Unravelling swiftly, it changed its shape to a tall man in a black cloak and a wide-brimmed hat. Dana didn't know he was called a *gruagach*, but she was glad he ignored her and strode away. A mountain hare exploded from a patch of heather. She was less surprised when it turned into a sharp-featured hag—she knew the superstition that hares were witches.

Here was the catch to Honor's gift. Did Dana really want to see what was all around her? There was a lot more than fairies at the bottom of the garden! Remembering the warning that not all would be friendly, she resumed her journey with a feeling of dread.

As she crossed a mountain stream flowing down a deep gully, she spied a woman kneeling on the rocks above. Where the woman dipped clothes in the water, the stream ran red. Dana shuddered. She recognized the *Bean Nighe*, the Washerwoman who scrubs the shrouds of the murdered. Her sister was the *Bean Sídhe*, the Banshee who howls at night over homes where someone will die. Quelling her horror, Dana hurried away. If only Gabriel were there, she could hold his hand tightly!

She travelled downhill, making her way through a patch of gorse. The thorny briars caught at her jeans and scraped her hands. When she heard the scampering noise behind her, she feared the worst. Fighting to stay calm, she peered into the bushes. A small creature hid there! She bit her lip. Stepped up her pace. Now the bushes on either side of her quivered. All the whin were moving and shaking. She choked with terror. There was a pack of them! She could bear it no longer.

She started to run.

CHAPTER Nine

Dana ran as fast as she could. Her heart was pounding. She gasped for breath. If only she had the hind's feet of the deer! If only she were safe at home! She could hear them behind her. Puffing and snorting. Little feet trampling. She barely kept her balance on the uneven ground. Patches of gorse stung and scratched her. Briars clawed and clutched her.

Something struck her from behind. She let out a cry. They were pelting her with stones! A shower of pebbles fell in front of her. Ancient pieces of flint, axe-heads like the ones in the museum. *Fairy arrows*, the old people called them, *elf-shots*.

It was the net that finally brought her down. Entangled in the woven rushes, she stumbled and fell. In an instant, they were all around her, squat little creatures with bog-coloured skin. She screamed and kicked and struggled wildly, but they managed to truss her up like a bundle. Hoisting her off the ground, they hurried down the mountain.

No one spoke directly to Dana, but they talked to each other, quick instructions and warnings. Their voices were murky and brackish.

"Puddle here!" one cried out on her right.

She was jerked sharply to the left.

"Muddy patch ahead!" someone called in front.

She was lifted up so suddenly that her stomach dropped.

"Patch of gorse! Up! Up!" came too late as thorns pricked her through the net.

"Ow! Be careful!" she yelled, but they ignored her.

Dana quelled her terror in an effort to keep her wits about her. She needed to know what they were and why they had kidnapped her. From time to time she put up a fight, lashing out to catch them by surprise, kicking and hitting from inside the net. Whenever she landed a blow or her foot met a soft body, they would shout or curse. But it only made them tighten their grip. Eventually she decided to conserve her strength and wait for a good moment to make her escape. Judging by the heaves and puffs, they were growing tired.

At one point, they halted abruptly together. A cuckoo's call had echoed from low ground. They waited for it to sound again and when it did, they cheered.

"'Twas on the right!"

"Good luck for a year and a day!"

They crowed with delight, then continued their march.

Evening was setting in. The light grew dim. The chill in the air had begun to bite. Despite the jiggling and jangling and her

unknown fate, Dana was beginning to find the journey monot-
onous. She had lost track of time. Had hours passed?

They were on new terrain. The feet of her captors squelched
in damp soil. When they dragged her over wet grass, Dana's
clothes got soaked. She noticed something else. They seemed to
have gained a second wind, jogging along at a lively pace. They
were also talking and laughing freely. Dana suspected they had
reached home ground.

"Isn't we the clever boggles? Our first human child stoled
in ages!"

"Ashah, they don't leaves their childer lying about any
more."

"True enough! No prams outside the house or under the
tree."

"No babbies on a blanket in the grass."

"No wains wandrin' to school through the fields on their
ownio."

"They guards them better nowadays."

"Feeds them better too!" a little voice piped up. "She be's
heavy! Five stone of praties at least."

"Aye, she be's a ton weight," another agreed breathlessly.
"The three-year-olds be best. She be's six or seven."

Though she had intended to keep quiet, this was too much
for Dana.

"I'm eleven!" she said indignantly.

A stony silence met her words. They were obviously
shocked.

"How is it she hear us, lads?"

"I knews she saw us! Not just the elf-stones."

"Some of thems could in the old days."

"She gots the right spirit. Wandrin' the hills all alone. Must be runnin' away from home."

"Well she be's far away now. We'll gets great sport from her."

They giggled and danced about, jigging her up and down.

"Ye means we're not going to eat her?"

The loud gasp from Dana led to more fits of laughter. She guessed (and hoped) they were joking. Still, she decided it was time to fight. With a great roar, she started to flail and kick and punch and scream. They were caught off guard. She was like a bag of cats. They dropped her on the ground. Fighting her way free of the net, Dana confronted her captors.

Boggles, they had called themselves, and to the bog they belonged. A muddy brown colour, they had long scrawny necks and plump heads and tummies. Their large webbed feet were flat as plates. Some were dour-looking and even grotesque, while others had scales that glittered like bronze. Their nicest feature were the big brown eyes that shone like copper pennies. They seemed curious and full of mischief, but not nasty or malign.

The boggles returned Dana's scrutiny with smug delight, nodding to each other and grinning and whispering. They were obviously sizing her up, pleased with their booty, their stolen prize. With a sinking feeling, Dana saw they had no fear of her escaping. When she looked around, she understood why.

They were standing in a vast bog that spread out on all sides as far as the eye could see. It was dreary and desolate. There was no sign of a road or cars or any human habitation. The sky was an immensity of twilight grey. The sodden ground was a sponge, drenched in mist. In the distance, she could see the dim outline of the mountains far away. Her heart sank. She was miles off course. Utterly lost. No wonder the boggles looked complacent.

She had nowhere to run.

CHAPTER TEN

A BOGGLE STEPPED
forward. He was obviously the leader, the biggest amongst them
at three feet in height. He was also the only one who appeared
to have hair, a bog asphodel growing from his head.

He bowed to Dana.

"We welcomes the human child to the Boglands. Can we
helps make your stay happy?"

"Leave me alone!" Dana screeched.

She lifted her foot to kick anyone who came near. They all
jumped back but weren't really alarmed. Some of them snickered.
They grinned at each other and shrugged, *well if that's the way she
wants it.* Drifting away in twos and threes, they skimmed over the
wet ground on their flat webbed feet like skaters on a pond.

When Dana saw they were deserting her, she panicked. She
had no idea where she was. Night was coming. She didn't want
to be left alone.

"Wait!" she called out. "Wait a minute!"

She hurried to catch up with them, but they ran away, scattering like sheep on the road.

"Come back," she shouted, chasing after them. "I won't fight, I promise!"

She had almost caught up with one and reached out to grab him, when he darted away at the last minute. They were all skittish and jumpy, squealing like piglets if she got too near. Some stopped to tease her, sticking out their tongues and thumbing their noses. Others cut capers, twirling around like whirligig beetles in a bog pool.

"Oh yeah?" Dana yelled at them. They were like the kids on her street. She couldn't ignore the challenge. "Oh yeah? I'll get you!"

She tore like the wind after the smallest boggle as the rest were too fast for her. At last she caught him.

"You're IT!" she roared with triumph.

He screeched with laughter and ran off to tackle the next target. The chase was on. A wild game of tag on the windswept bog. They raced over hummocks of deergrass and hollows of heather. Splashed through pools choked with sphagnum mosses. Scrambled over high ridges of turf. The soft ground or *bogach* that gave the land its name squelched underfoot. They were soon covered in muck.

Hiccuping with laughter, Dana was lost in the fun. It was wonderful just to be a kid again, to run and jump, to topple and tumble, to forget about missions and missing mothers and fathers left behind in Bray.

The game switched to leap-frog. Dana's long legs made her

the fastest. When the boggles declared her the winner, she jumped up and down with glee.

"They soon forgets they's human," one of the boggles said to another.

Dana overheard his words and felt a twinge of foreboding. In the back of her mind she knew something was wrong. She shrugged it off. If she was in trouble, she would face the music later. Right now, she wanted to play.

One of the boggles scrambled up a bank of peat.

"I's the King of the Castle!" he proclaimed.

Another knocked him down.

"And I's the Dirty Rascal!"

The sun was sinking in the western mountains. The bog shone like bronze. The evening air swarmed with midges and the iridescent flies named after dragons and damsels. The fragrant scent of bog myrtle wafted on the breeze. As darkness set in, a change came over the boggles. Where their eyes were the colour of copper in daylight, they glowed like gold coins under the moon.

They continued to play out in the dark till Dana was cold and hungry and drenched to the skin. She started to shiver. A chill wind was blowing over the landscape. At last the boggles called a halt to the games and built a bonfire of bog oak and turf. Sweet-smelling flames and bursts of red sparks lit up the night.

One of the gang, Dana sat in the circle around the fire. Clothes caked in mud, dark curls plastered to her forehead, she argued with the others about who won which game. As it was almost impossible to tell one boggle from another, she would confuse their names. Each time she apologized, they pooh-poohed her regrets.

"We understands," explained Piper, the leader. "Humans looks alike to us. Unless they's different colours. We likes the brown ones best."

Aside from the leader, the smallest boggle was the easiest to recognize as his name was Bird and he had a beak for a nose. But she would never be able to tell the difference between Butterhill and Silverhill, who were twin brothers, or Snow and Twig, who were not related but looked identical. Then there was Underhill who was no relation to the two other "hills" but was a cousin of Goodfellow, Lightbow and Gem. Some boggles could be identified by what they wore. Green did dress all in green while Stone wore a little chain of pebbles round his neck.

When a big cauldron was set in the middle of the fire, ingredients for a stew were tossed in willy-nilly. Mouth-watering smells filled the air. Dana looked curiously into the pot at the flora of the bog bubbling there: dark-purple liverworts as fat as worms, green and black moss, leathery bogbean with fleshy stems and hairy flowers, bottle sedge and pondweed with flat red leaves. She wondered a moment if it were safe to eat, then decided she didn't care. She was ravenous after the day's adventures. No time to be fussy.

While the bog bouillabaisse brewed, Dana shared out her chocolates. Since no one told them not to, they ate dessert first. At last the stew was ready and dished out in wooden bowls. It was truly scrumptious. Dana felt she was eating the bog itself. The chief taste was "brown," reminding her of all the brown things she liked best: fried mushrooms, HP Sauce, wholemeal soda bread and the crisp skins of potatoes baked in the oven. They offered her brackish water to drink, but she declined.

When she passed around the bottle of cola, they admired the colour but spat it out.

"You probably don't like chemicals," said Dana.

"You does?!"

"Yeah, tastes great."

They huddled around the fire, leaning against each other, a bunch of mucky kids with dirty faces. Dana felt like Wendy with Peter Pan's lost boys. Now that things had grown quiet, she was returning to herself. She was beginning to remember why she was out in the mountains.

"Okay, lads," she announced. "Time to get serious. There's something—"

Before she could finish, the boggles were on their feet. The moon had risen to light up the bog like a shining playground.

"Time to dance!" they cried.

The boggles skipped over the coarse ground as if it were a smooth floor. Some played reed pipes and round skin drums. As the wild music echoed over the landscape, they footed with glee.

Despite her protests, Dana found herself in the centre of a ring. *Celebrate the Kidnapped Child Dance* entailed throwing her into the air, again and again. Her stomach hurt from laughing so much but at last the boggles' arms grew tired.

For *The Dance of Lights* each picked a star and, keeping their eye on it, spun madly around. When the music halted, all came to a stop except the sky and earth, which kept on turning. They staggered around whooping till they all fell down.

Crack the Whip had them holding hands in a long line, careering recklessly across the bog, zigging and zagging so sharply that those at the end had to cling on for dear life. This was the dance, known to Dana as a game, that brought them to the crossroads.

Dana hadn't noticed they were skipping along a road that bordered the bog like a river. The signpost gave her a jolt. She had forgotten human things and was startled to see it. In her surprise, she let go of the whip and went flying headfirst into a ditch. Scrambling out, she ran back to the crossroads.

The black-and-white signs pointed in the four directions. Dublin to the north. Glendalough and Laragh to the south. Blessington to the west. Bray to the east. Now she knew where she was. In the Sally Gap. High up in the eastern reaches of the mountains. Way off course! Miles behind in the wrong direction! It all came flooding back. What she had forgotten as she played. Her mission. Her mother. Her reason for leaving her poor father.

A familiar sound in the distance made Dana turn. She saw the headlights of a car, approaching slowly.

The boggles had also spotted the car and were instantly alert. They didn't want their fun to end. The whip cracked back towards Dana to grab hold of her. Howling like a war party, they scurried away, off the road and back into the bog.

The Triumph Herald stopped at the crossroads. Gabriel got out and looked around.

"There's nothing here," Aradhana called gently from the car.

"I'm sure I saw something," Gabriel muttered.

He rubbed his head. His eyes looked haunted. Was he chasing shadows? But he had to do something. Rescue teams were combing the mountains. The police helicopter was out. Still no sign of her. Gabriel knew what had happened. She had run away, to protest against the move to Canada. He was sick with guilt and worry. What if something terrible happened to her? He couldn't, wouldn't rest until he found her.

Where could she be?

CHAPTER ELEVEN

İt was well past midnight.
The bog lay dark and still beneath a starry sky. Dana lounged
with the boggles around the campfire, gazing upwards. Whenever a star fell in a silver streak, they would cry out together,
"What is the stars? What is the stars?"

In the hiatus between games, Dana thought hard and fast.
She had finally figured it out. Lost in play, she became one of
them. She only returned to herself when they took a rest. She
wasn't afraid, she considered the boggles harmless, but she
would have to outwit them.

Bird climbed into her lap like a toddler and offered her a
sundew, a carnivorous bog plant with whiskery legs.

"Say 'for a year and a day I promise to stay,'" he implored her.

She smiled down at the big golden eyes, met the eager
looks of the others around her. They were such funny little
things. She really liked them.

All held their breath as Dana took the sundew and stared at it gingerly. At last she spoke in a solemn tone:

For a year and a day
I promise to stay.

They were about to cheer when she added quickly:

—No way!
But I promise to stay
For the rest of the day.

So let there be no sorrow
When I leave tomorrow.
Though we'll say goodbye
Our friendship won't die.

It was such a good trick, they had to applaud. The matter was settled then. She would stay the night and go in the morning. They showed her where she would sleep. Burrows had been dug throughout the bog. Called a *pollach* or bog-hole, each was a snug little space deep underground with a bend in the tunnel to keep out the rain. Lined with fresh rushes and tufts of white bog cotton, they reminded Dana of her hamsters' nests.

Back at the campfire, the boggles relaxed as they no longer had to distract her with continuous games. Instead they told stories of their mischief and mayhem. How they knocked down stone walls, stole clothes off washing lines, turned over

dustbins and potted plants. Their favourite prank, they con-
fessed, was blowing wind down the chimney till a cloud of soot
shrouded the house.

"The housewifes does wail like the Banshee!" they cried
gleefully.

Dana tried not to laugh at their antics, but she couldn't help
it. They were so like bold boys, homeless, motherless, and badly
needing attention.

"I never heard of boggles before," she told them, "only the
bogeyman."

They all shuddered.

"Don't mentions him! He scares us too!"

"Black sheep of the family! Black Bart the Bogeyman!"

They counted on their fingers and toes the different mem-
bers of the Clan Boggle: boggles of course, bogles, boggarts,
bogeys, bloody-bones, brownies, bugbears, hobgoblins, boggy-
boes, dobbies, hobthrusts, hobby-lanthorns, tantarrabobs,
hodge-podgers, bolls, bomen, brags, flay-boggarts, peg-powlers,
pucks, madcaps, buggaboes, clabbernappers, gnomes, thrummy
caps, spriggans and kobolds, who were German relations.

"So many kinds and nobody ever sees them!" was Dana's
comment.

"We stays in the mountains and far-off places."

"You's seen the leprechauns, I bets. Lots of them moves to
the town. They passes for humans."

"No, I've never—" Dana began, then she stopped. She suddenly remembered all the times she *had* seen them, those little
old men sitting on the bus or standing at the street corner. The
one who found her a seat in the coffee shop. The other one

who gave her a book in the library—about fairies! of course! All those little old men with knobbly noses and hairy ears and twinkling eyes. Each time she had seen them, she had thought to herself, *he looks like a leprechaun.*

They had reached that time of the night when friendship was close and secrets were shared. Dana finally asked the question she was dying to ask.

"Are there any girl boggles?"

Their response was as swift and abrupt as a blow. Bird scampered out of her lap. Everyone recoiled. Some began to fidget. Many looked away. Others busied themselves tending the fire. They became not only taciturn but deeply sad.

"We don't talks about them," Piper said at last. He stared dismally into the flames. "Our Ivy and Sally, our Flower and Pepper."

"Our Megs and Mags and Pegs and Pogs."

"Our Dew and Dally and Sue and Tally."

"We misses our girls!"

"Off they went and it had to be."

"All alone are we!"

Their big golden eyes went dim and watery like the moon on a lake. They started to sniff. Then great tears rolled down their cheeks and off their noses, splashing into the fire with a hiss.

"I'm so sorry!" Dana cried. "I should've minded my own business. I didn't mean to upset you!"

Now they wept and howled. Dana felt like a babysitter who has lost control of her charges, all wailing for their mother.

"They'll return one day," she said desperately.

"Not till the light comes back," sobbed little Bird.

As soon as the words were uttered, the others snapped out of their woe. Those nearest to Bird clapped their hands on his mouth.

"Say nothing!"

"Whispers gets carried by the wind!"

"If he hears, he wakes!"

Dana was alert to the new shift in mood. The air was fraught with tension.

"Who might hear? Do you have an enemy?"

They shook their heads furiously. Their mouths clammed shut. She tried to think of a way to reach them. Something niggled at the back of her mind. Bird had mentioned "the light." Could it have anything to do with her mission?

"Do you know Lugh of the Mountain?" she asked.

"Lugh of the Wood?" they cried in chorus.

All froze in their places, except Piper, the leader. He stood up stiffly.

"Why do you asks?"

His voice was so taut it almost squeaked. Dana was wary. Their mood had changed again. They were all regarding her with deep suspicion.

"I've a message for him," she explained hesitantly. "From the High King of—"

Before she could finish they were wailing again, this time in terror.

"The Gentry has sent her!"

"After we kepts them away!"

"The tricksters! To send a human child!"

"How coulds we know?"

Their dread was terrible to behold. Bold children, indeed, suddenly caught out and deathly afraid of punishment.

"What cans we do?"

"If she finds him, she wakes him."

"All the storms! All the rain!"

"Our *pollach*s drownded!"

"There mights be floods!"

"There mights be a BOG-BURST!"

They worked themselves into a frenzy till the wails reached a crescendo and broke into silence. The eyes that glared at Dana went cold as metal. She sensed their ill will and grew afraid.

"We must keeps her from him!"

"We must hides her away!"

Dana didn't try to plead or argue. Too much had changed too quickly. They had become her enemy. Acting on instinct, she jumped up from the fire and ran like mad.

They ran after her, flat feet skating over the bog. But she wasn't as easy to catch this time. Thanks to their games, she knew the ground and the drier paths. She saw the grey ribbon of road in the distance, saw the pale yellow lamps of a car drawing near. Waving her arms, she screamed for help.

Too late. Once again, the net fell over her and she was caught in its web.

"Let me go!" she begged, as they hauled her back to their campsite. "I thought we were friends. I wouldn't do anything to harm you!"

Her pleas fell on deaf ears. They dragged her to an empty *pollach* on the far side of the bog.

"Don't do this!" she cried, as they forced her inside and rolled a stone against the entrance.

"We must," they finally answered before they left her. "We has no choice! We hast to do it!"

She heard the regret in their voices. Little Bird was crying. But no one moved to help her.

"We must keeps you away from Lugnaquillia. Let sleeping dogs lie. Lugh must not wake!"

They left her in that deserted place, in the black of night. Her cries for help echoed over the bleak landscape.

But no one heard. She was all alone.

CHAPTER TWELVE

DANA HUDDLED ON THE
ground, a bundle of misery. She had shouted for help till she was
hoarse. Though she was trying to be brave, the tears trickled
down. She wished she had never met Honor, never agreed to
the mission, never run away from home. Once she started to cry,
she couldn't stop. Finally, drained and exhausted, she fell asleep.

Dana woke in her bed in Wolfe Tone Square. Gabriel was
standing over her with a cup of warm milk.

"You had another nightmare," he said gently. "I'll stay
beside you."

So it was just a dream! Happy and relieved, she drank the
milk and went back to sleep while her father watched over her.

When Dana woke again in the cold dark *pollach*, it was all
the worse. She was stiff and sore. The air smelled stale. Since the
boggles had taken her knapsack, she had nothing to eat or drink.
Would she die in this place? She was about to start crying again,

when she heard something beneath her. She pressed her ear to the ground. Faint echoes of music and revelry. The boggles? Unlikely. Though they slept underground, they lived in the open.

A tapping sound came from the wall beside her. A crack veined the clay, then slowly widened, parting the wall. Golden light poured through the seam along with the sweetest music imaginable. Dana pressed her face to the crack to peer inside.

There, before her eyes, a miniature world unfolded. A subterranean country of wonders and delights. She saw trees blossoming with fruits and flowers, golden castles atop green hills, swans gliding over mirror lakes, comely people riding to sport with falcons on their wrists. Now the view changed to a marbled hall. Richly clad lords and ladies were feasting and dancing within. Some sat at a banquet table, raising jewelled cups to toast. Others twirled over the floor to the music of a waltz. Dana felt like a child at the window of a sweet shop. How she longed to be in there!

Unaware of the breach in their world, the shining company took no notice of Dana. Then one little fellow, no more than a boy, came hurrying towards her. His behaviour was furtive, he kept looking around him. Under his short cape, he hid a gold cup. When he reached Dana, he smiled and bowed, then thrust the goblet at her. Dana caught the faint whiff of blackberry and cinnamon before the cup transformed. In her hand was an acorn filled with dew.

The boy beckoned, urging her to join him.

"I can't," she said in despair. "I'm too big. I won't fit."

He motioned her to drink.

Dana froze for a moment. The old tales warned against eating or drinking. How could she know if he were friend or foe? Her situation was bad, but might it get worse?

"Follow the greenway," he whispered.

Like a secret password, the words assured her. A message from Honor? She downed the acorn in one sup. The effect was instant. Dana began to shrink and shrivel like a dried-up leaf. It was the oddest sensation. She thought of Alice in Wonderland and was glad the potion hadn't made her bigger! The *pollach* was now an immense cavern, while the crack was a grand archway into the marbled hall.

As Dana stepped inside, the music swelled around her like an orchestra. A party of revellers spun past and caught her up in their circle. It was some kind of nature dance. They wove in and out, plaiting together oak leaves and ivy, tufts of fleece and twigs. Something was slowly taking shape in their midst. A finely wrought cradle? Or was it a boat? Dana was about to ask one of her partners, when a dancer in a mask clasped her hand.

"Come away," she whispered urgently.

Dana recognized Honor's voice. The young woman was radiant in a sky-blue gown with a silver cloak and feathered mask. Her hair was braided with strings of pearls.

She drew Dana away from the crowd.

"I thought you couldn't come here!" said Dana, surprised.

"I've broken the rules!" Honor was breathless with excitement. "For your sake, my human self defies Faerie! Except for my page, who brought you here, the others do not even know where we are. I have brought the entire court! It was the only way to do it without anyone's heed."

Dana was amazed.

"How can they not know?!"

"I've brought the whole place—lock, stock and barrel. We could be anywhere in Ireland! And they're all immersed in their game. We're weaving a robin's nest for one whose mate has been injured. The High King is away in the North. He's the only one I couldn't deceive."

Even through the mask, Dana could see the mischief sparkling in Honor's eyes. Not for the first time, she realized that fairies enjoyed being bold!

"We must hurry!" Honor finished quickly. "Time grows short. I have remembered something I need to tell you."

She took Dana's hand and rushed her from the hall, down a flight of stairs that led deep underground.

"I came not only to free you," Honor explained, "but also to warn you. There was something I forgot in my confusion of self. I promised you your heart's desire, but know this. As you are of Wicklow, it is King Lugh who must grant the boon and you must ask it of him on his feast day, *Lá Lughnasa*."

"*Lá* means day," Dana said, quickly translating the Irish. "*Lughnasa* is August. August day. The first?"

"Yes!" said Honor. "Lammas. You must reach Lugnaquillia by then. Once you have given the message, you can make your wish."

"That's the day after tomorrow!" Dana exclaimed. Her face creased with worry. "Things are already worse. The king is fast asleep, under some kind of spell. It's the boggles who have been keeping everyone out. They don't want you to wake him."

"The boggles!" Honor was astonished. "Why would they?

How could they? They're harmless creatures! Oh, I know they kidnapped you, but they were just being naughty. They would never have harmed you."

Dana was hardly convinced and was about to argue, when they reached the end of the steps. Before them lay the beautiful landscape she had first spied through the crack. The Summer Country. The Plain of the Apple Trees. The Many-Coloured Land.

"Is this Faerie?"

"Yes," said Honor blithely. "And no. Faerie is everywhere and anywhere, every shape and any thing. This is an aspect of Faerie, the favourite of the court. I had to move *everything* to allay suspicion."

Dana was awed by what her friend had done, but worried too.

"What if you get caught! Won't they turn you into a frog or something? I don't want you to get into trouble for helping me."

"It's the least I can do! I am ashamed that they . . . that we . . . do not aid you more. While I would never regret belonging to them, there are many things about the fairies I find hard to accept. They aren't like us, you know."

Dana was struck by Honor's strange situation: half in, half out, half this, half that. Even the way she spoke seemed betwixt and between.

"Did they steal you when you were small?"

Honor let out a little sigh.

"It's a long story, Dana, the length of a book. Perhaps one day you'll hear it. But for now, we must away!"

With Honor still holding Dana's hand, they were suddenly

running as fast as the wind. The multicoloured country hurtled past them, like scenery from the window of a passing train. Then just as suddenly they came to a halt. Dana's stomach lurched.

They were on a wide green, in the midst of a country fair. Tents and stalls dotted the grass. Crowds milled about, gaily dressed in high crowned hats and colourful cloaks. Many of the fairgoers looked human, but there were also giants and dwarves and other strange creatures. Inside the tents, contests and entertainments were taking place: acrobatics and singing, theatre and dancing, magic and recitation. A strong lady lifted iron weights. An old man swallowed swords of fire. The booths outdoors sold every kind of ware: bolts of rich fabric, heaps of precious stones, cakes and sweets, mechanical toys. Mouth-watering smells wafted from the food stalls where delicious treats sizzled and spat in great pans.

Dana stared around, wide-eyed. Honor gave her a velvet purse bulging with coins.

"Buy yourself some new clothes—you're covered in bog mud! And provisions for travelling. You must haggle for the price or they will cheat you, especially the cluricauns. They're the ones with the red noses."

"Haggle?" Dana was horrified. She would rather face danger than argue over prices.

"You can do it," Honor insisted. Her tone was that of a big sister. "I must return to court before they note my absence. I'll be back as soon as I can. Shop till you drop!"

Dana wandered from stall to stall, tempted by all the knick-knacks, geegaws and gimcracks. She had never seen so many outlandish and fascinating things. Could she make use of a bracelet that would turn her purple? Or a ball that bounced as high as the clouds? With an effort, she remembered what she had to do.

"Out dancing under the moon with boggles, I see!" snorted the leprechaun at the cobblers' stall.

She had brought him her running shoes, waterlogged and caked with mud.

The fat little shoemaker had a round red face with a red beard and red hair that sprouted from his head, nose and ears. He wore a leather apron with pockets full of nails. Nails also stuck out of his mouth like a pincushion, as he tapped away with his hammer. He scraped, sewed, buffed and polished her shoes, complaining throughout about her lack of care. When he was finished, they looked brand new. Feeling ashamed and guilty, Dana gave him a large gold coin for his efforts. He bit it, looked pleased and even mollified. Before she took back her shoes, he drove a tiny silver nail into the sole of each.

"That will help ye run faster." He winked. "But stay off the bogs!"

Next, Dana bought herself new clothes for travelling. Keeping in mind the chill of the mountains, she chose blue woollen trousers, a cambric shirt, a knitted vest, and a long green cloak with a hood. She also bought a satchel and filled it with provisions: apples and oranges, curranty bread, a chunk of cheese, fairy buns with icing, and a big bottle of ginger wine.

Honor found her at the sweet stall, mesmerized by the array of candies and ices. Dana had already bought a red licorice as long as her arm. Should she go for the exploding chocolate as well?

"Chocolate's the best treat here," Honor advised. "It's a fairy invention, you know. A mortal called Willie stole the recipe."

Dana showed off her purchases. The older girl praised her choices but was shocked at the prices.

"You were robbed!" she cried. "The bold things!"

Laughing and chatting, they left the fairgreen. As the merry sounds faded behind them, Dana grew quiet. She had enjoyed the shopping and Honor's company. After so much fun, she was not looking forward to wandering through the mountains on her own again.

A great arch loomed on the road ahead: two giant standing stones with a cap stone on top. Dana knew what it was. There were dolmens and cromlechs all over Ireland. Many believed they were portals to other worlds.

Honor saw the glum look on the younger girl's face. Her eyes filled with pity.

"You don't have to go back," she said softly. "You can change your mind, especially now, as you know how difficult it can be. Say but the word and I shall send you through this gateway, not to the mountains, but home instead."

Dana was sorely tempted. The mission was certainly harder and more complicated than she had expected. It was also lonely and scary, not to mention dangerous. On top of all that, she was really worried about Gabriel and missing him badly.

On the other hand, would she be happy if she backed out now? It was all so exciting. The greatest adventure she had ever had! The more she survived, the stronger she felt and the more she believed she could actually do it. Her dream was possible.

She could accomplish the mission and earn her wish to find her mother.

Something else inspired Dana. She had seen a lot of Faerie and the more she knew of it, she more she liked it. Despite its bad points, it was a precious place, beautiful and magical and well worth helping. There was also her friendship with Honor, which was growing steadily. Dana didn't want to let her down.

"Thanks for the choice," said Dana. "It makes things clearer. I don't want to go home. Not till I've done what I came here to do."

Honor regarded her proudly.

"The longing for home is the hero's greatest obstacle. You do well to overcome it, you gain in strength. I have no doubt you will succeed in your quest."

"Will this gateway bring me to Lugnaquillia?"

"If it were only that simple!" Honor sighed. "But there are some rules not even a High King could subvert. This is your journey, Dana, not mine. I cannot bring you to your goal, I can only help you on your way."

She pulled up Dana's hood and tucked the dark curls inside.

"Listen carefully, dear heart. As you pass through the dolmen, call on the gods of your people. It is your birthright. Call for a guide and companion."

The two girls hugged like sisters.

"Thank you," Dana said. "Thanks for all your help."

"No, no, thank *you*," said Honor. "Thanks for all *your* help."

Dana stepped through the archway. The stones began to glow and hum. As if from far away, she heard a faint singing.

The voice was silvery and musical. She thought it was Honor,
but she wasn't sure.

> *Fare you well, traveller*
> *As you journey to the light.*
> *The land of your wish lies waiting*
> *At the other end of night.*

CHAPTER THiRTEEN

As Dana stepped through the dolmen, she did as Honor told her. She called out with all her heart and soul for help on her quest. When she arrived on the other side, she was back in the mountains, restored to her own height. It was early dawn. The sun was rising. The hills were a rose-coloured sea tinged with gold.

She stood on a jagged peak, overlooking a steep slope covered with stones and broken boulders. The talus of scree fell to a half-moon of white sand that shored a deep lake. She could see the smoke of a campfire on the beach far below. With a thrill, she recognized Lough Dan, named after the goddess Danu for whom she also was named. She was back on track. If she kept a steady pace, she was sure to reach Lugnaquillia in time for *Lá Lughnasa*, two days away.

"The sun rises in the east," she reminded herself and set off in the opposite direction, westwards.

She was far up in the mountains. Neither the Wicklow Way nor the trekkers who hiked it came this far. Her only company were the red grouse scrabbling in the heather and a herd of feral goats treading the narrow crags. High in the air came the occasional *kee kee* cry of the peregrine falcon, Lord of the Hills.

Though the mountain wind blew incessantly, Dana was snug in her fairy clothes. The green cloak swirled around her like wings. Her running shoes seemed hardly to touch the ground.

As she travelled downhill, the terrain grew more habitable. The stony ground softened to sedge and moorgrass. Before her lay the valley of Glenmacnass, a green bowl set in the dark rim of hills. To her right fell a waterfall in gentle decline over rocks and rushes, winding through the glen like a silver ribbon. To her left, higher up and opposite the river, ran a grey strip of road.

An early morning mist drifted through the glen. The sun was warm on her face, the breeze cool on her skin. Dana hurried for the woods that bordered the river. She knew friends of Gabriel's owned the farm nearby. Their sheep, daubed with red paint, grazed the hillside. She didn't feel safe till she reached the shelter of the trees.

It was an old spinney, mostly oak in full leaf. A silver-green moss clung to bole and branch. Light glimmered in green shadows. Fiddlehead fern curled in the undergrowth. A still and magical place, perfect for a picnic. Dana sat on a tree stump to have her breakfast.

As she ate her cheese and apples, she looked around her happily. That's when she saw them. Everywhere. Flower fairies, like multicoloured butterflies, flitted over the foxglove and woodbine, daisy and wild rose. Deep in the trees, a lady stepped lithely. Dana thought at first she was Honor, but there was nothing human about her at all. She had bark-brown skin and green hair like ivy. The wind whispered her name as she walked. *Greensleeves.* Now Dana turned at the sound of a galloping horse. A dark man in a black cloak rode past on a night mare. From his saddlebag he tossed glittering dust in the air. Wherever the dust landed, mushrooms sprang up—elf-caps, yellow fairy clubs and red-and-white fly agaric.

The more she saw the more Dana understood how the two worlds intertwined, the part that Faerie played in nature. She found herself wondering, if the countryside disappeared would Faerie die too? Now she remembered what Honor had said, the first time they met in the Glen of the Downs. *The destruction of the forest is the beginning of the end of our world.*

Her meal finished, Dana was more eager than ever to resume her mission. The desire to succeed for Faerie's sake kept growing inside her. Come hell or high water, the King of Wicklow would get his message.

She hadn't gone far into the woods when the leaves started to hiss.

Elm do grieve
Oak do hate
Willow do walk
If you travel late.

Dana shivered. It was an ominous whisper, cold and unfriendly. At the corner of her eye, she saw a tree move. A weeping willow. Its roots seemed to wade through the soil as if it were water.

Willow do walk
If you travel late.

"It's not late!" Dana called nervously.

The willow promptly planted itself down. Something about its offended air made Dana wonder if it weren't trying to warn her.

Moments later, she knew it was.

Oak do hate.

She was surrounded by oak trees, hemming her in on all sides. Then she realized they weren't trees at all, but arboreal giants. Gnarled and knobbled with bark for skin, they had leaf-green hair and dark knots for eyes. They tramped towards her with wooden clubs.

Oakmen do hate.

She sensed their malevolence. They hated humans. Humans killed trees. An image flashed through her mind. The Glen of the Downs. Trees marked with white paint, tagged for felling. *An eye for an eye. A tooth for a tooth.* The dream of Faerie had become a nightmare.

Dana wanted to protest that she was only a child, that she had done her best as an eco-warrior. But they were not there to listen. She had to flee. Spying a weak spot in their advance, she charged wildly towards them and ducked under their arms.

It was a mad dash, a hopeless hurtle. Expecting to be clubbed at any moment, she screamed as she ran.

To Dana's surprise, she cleared the Oakmen easily. They stamped and crashed behind her like falling trees. As she fled through the forest, she found herself dodging and darting much faster than usual. The gift of the leprechaun! The silver nails in her shoes! Hope surged through her. She had a good chance. The trees were thinning out ahead. She was near the edge of the forest. Would they dare to pursue her into the open?

But now as her safety seemed assured, Dana gasped with new terror. There before her, blocking her path, stood another enemy—fierce and ravenous, fangs bared and snarling.

A huge wolf.

The great shaggy beast was as tall as Dana. Its yellow eyes glared like the sun. Rising on its haunches with a powerful vault, it leaped towards her.

There was no time to think. No time to run. No time even to cry out.

Dana felt a moment of indescribable fear. The threat of extinction. Time itself seemed to slow and stretch. The grey streak of animal made an arc through the air. The yellow eyes narrowed like two crescent moons. The red jaw gaped. A deadly calm came over Dana. A calm that seemed strangely to come from the wolf itself. The splendour of that leap. The cry of the wild. Despite the fear, something thrilled inside her. A thought entered her mind, perhaps her last. If this was how she would die, it was a noble death.

But she was wrong.

The wolf continued its flight over Dana's head to attack the Oakmen. Stunned, she turned to watch. The Oakmen roared with fury, striking out with their clubs, but they were too slow for the beast. Their clubs beat the earth without landing a blow. The wolf bit and clawed. The Oakmen howled.

Dana knew she should run while both her enemies were busy, yet she hesitated. Though she suspected the wolf was just guarding its dinner, she couldn't be sure. What if it were trying to save her? She had seen a program about wolves, they rarely attacked humans. She was vaguely aware of something else, some bond with the wolf she couldn't explain. To run away seemed the act of a coward. She looked around for a weapon.

But the battle was over. The last Oakman fled through the trees. The great wolf stood alone, snapping and snarling. Now it turned to Dana.

The moment of truth. Child and beast confronted each other. *What a beautiful face*, Dana thought. It had the smooth snout of a great dog, finely pricked ears and golden eyes. Though her legs went weak, Dana stood her ground. Again, a strange calm descended upon her. She wasn't surprised when the wolf spoke.

"Do you know who I am?"

The words came through a growl, low and deep. The voice was female.

Dana was thrilled to the core of her being. She could hardly speak.

"You are the wolf."

The she-wolf tossed her great head.

"In the tongue of your people, what is my name?"

Dana was confused for a minute, then understood the question.

"You are the *faol*."

The wolf padded softly towards her.

"Think, little cub. Why does the feeling of kinship conquer your fear?"

Dana caught her breath. The truth struck her like a burst of light, a surge of joy.

"I am a *Faolán*. I belong to you."

Chapter Fourteen

THE SHE-WOLF GROWLED her approval.

"And I to you. I am the guardian of your clan. The totem of your tribe. You called for help, I have come to guide you."

Dana knew the wolf's words were true. In the mists of time, the earliest peoples of Ireland were named for the animals from whom they believed they descended. The oldest families still had those names, anglicized as the mother tongue declined. Whelans. Whalens. Phelans. Phalens. All were *Faoláns*. Of the Clan of the Wolf.

"If you were fully grown," the wolf told her, "I would tear out your throat and savage your limbs. I would dismember you and then restore you. In doing this, I would tear from you what makes you weak, what holds you back. You would be a wolf. But you are only a cub. Hard lessons must wait."

Dana straightened her back. She had cried out to the gods

of her people, and the guardian of her tribe had answered the call. A great honour had been granted her. She stared at the lolling tongue and the sharp canine teeth. She did not feel like Little Red Riding Hood. She did not want a forester to save her, to kill the wolf. Indeed, she would have fought the forester herself to defend the guardian. She thought of her quest. How hard it was proving. All her faltering and failing. She made up her mind.

"I want to be a wolf," she said. "I don't care how young I am. Tear me apart. Make me strong."

The wolf barked a deep laugh. She was huge in both height and bulk. She lifted her head. The fangs were so near it seemed she might allow Dana's request. Her breath was gamey, wild and invigorating. But she didn't bite. She licked Dana's face as she would lick a cub.

"Adults must be torn apart because life defeats them. They lose hope, they grow weak. They squander their inheritance. Children need not be torn, for they hold to their birthright. Their hearts are as wild as the hearts of birds. They have the courage of the wolf."

Dana understood. Though Gabriel was strong and brave, she was stronger and braver. He had been defeated by the loss of his wife. He had given up. He had stopped searching for her. That was why Dana had to take up the mission. She had to do what her father had failed to do.

"Listen to me, little wolf. Time grows short. The shadow of the Enemy is crossing the land. It draws near to you even as you draw near to the light and it will try to stop you from accomplishing your mission."

Dana shivered as if something cold had gripped her.

"Honor mentioned the same thing, the shadow, the Enemy. It's part of my message, but I didn't think it had anything to do with me. It's Faerie's problem, isn't it?"

The wolf's gaze was steady.

"You already suspect the truth, little cub. The two worlds are not separate. They intertwine. What affects the one, affects the other. Of the shadow and the Enemy, you will learn more in time, but not now, not here. Today we run."

With that, the wolf vaulted into the air. In a spectacular manoeuvre of power and grace, she spun right around to land back on all fours.

"Follow the greenway!" she cried to Dana. "Run wild, run free!"

Though she ran on two legs, Dana felt she had four. The power of the wolf had pervaded her limbs with sleek sinews, strong muscle and great lolloping gait. They crossed the Glenmacnass River in a spray of cold water. Dashed through the woods that lined the scarp. Up, up the steep side of Brockagh Mountain, then across its bare summit.

To run with the deer had been sweetness and light, a gentle union with nature, soft grass and sunshine. *Blessed are the meek.* To run with the wolf was to run in the shadows, the dark ray of life, survival and instinct. A fierceness that was proud and lonely, a tearing, a howling, a hunger and thirst. *Blessed are they who hunger and thirst.* A strength that would die fighting, kicking, screaming, that wouldn't stop till the last breath had been wrung from its body. The will to take one's place in the world. To say *I am here.* To say *I am.*

They travelled for miles before they stopped for a break. It was late afternoon. They were high in the mountains, on a bleak plateau.

"What meat have you?" asked the wolf eagerly as Dana dug in her satchel.

"None. I'm a vegetarian."

She spread out the bread, cheese and apples.

"A herbivore? Your teeth are those of a flesh-eater, like myself!"

Dana mumbled through a mouthful of sandwich.

"I won't eat anything that had a face. I love animals."

The she-wolf shook her head, mystified. She chomped on an apple, nosed around under rocks for insects, then loped away without a word.

Dana stayed where she was to finish her lunch. But when she heard the cry in the distance, a bird or small animal, she couldn't ignore it. She hurried towards the sound.

"Oh how could you!" she cried.

There stood the wolf, in a patch of heather, over the remains of a wild rabbit. Blood smeared her snout and the greenery around her. She was chewing raw meat.

"The poor little thing!" Dana wept, thinking of her own beloved pet. "How could you be so evil!"

Licking her chops, the wolf regarded the rest of her meal. Then she trained her golden gaze on Dana.

"I honour the creature who dies that I may live. In turn, I shall die for the life of another one day. It is the Great Round." She let out a low growl. "Climb on my back. I will show you evil that you may know the difference."

Though she was angry and upset, Dana did as she was told. It was like riding a small pony who could run like a racehorse. She buried her hands in the warm fur of the wolf's neck and held on tightly. The land blurred as they moved.

They came down from the mountains, from the solitary byways, to travel through areas where humans dwelled. Dana was alarmed at the sight of tilled fields and farmhouses, meadows with cattle and pine plantations. In such occupied places, they could easily get caught. She got a shock when she saw her own face on a poster tacked to a telephone pole. MISSING CHILD. REWARD.

They arrived at last at a forest marked with signs that said WILDLIFE SANCTUARY. The wolf bade Dana slide off her back.

"Follow me," she murmured.

They crept through the trees, hunkering in the underbrush as the wolf led the way. Dana heard the laughter first, then she saw them. Three men around a campfire, drinking beer. Empty cans were strewn on the ground around them, but it wasn't at the cans that Dana stared in horror.

Wire cages were stacked against the trees. Each was crammed with terrified rabbits. All had been trapped and wounded, their fur streaked with blood. Some were half-dead, kicking feebly. Even as she watched them, images flashed through Dana's mind. Trucks jammed with cattle, sheep and horses crossing Europe without food or water. Battery hens locked in boxes for life, laying eggs till they died, never once having seen either grass or sky. Crates of animals, from little mice to great apes, unloaded at laboratories for torture and testing. And amongst those scenes of cruelty and suffering, she also saw people. Trainloads of men, women and children with yellow stars on their chests.

Dana thought her heart would break.

"There is no respect for life in the shadow of the Enemy," the wolf said beside her.

Dana returned to herself. The poachers were joking about their catch as they cleaned their snares for resetting. She felt sick to her stomach, but she was also enraged. Without thinking, she ran out to confront them.

"Can you not *see*? The pain right in front of you? The suffering you're causing?"

The men jumped up in fright. Was there an adult with her? Maybe the game warden? Then one lurched forward to peer drunkenly at Dana.

"It's the missing kid from Bray! There's a reward for her!"

The fear in their faces turned quickly to greed. Dana stepped back, suddenly aware of their size, of her own vulnerability. They stepped menacingly towards her. She was about to turn and run when the men stopped abruptly. They were looking beyond her, eyes glazed with terror. Dana heard the growl, as the wolf reared up.

The poachers ran screaming into the woods. Dana raced to release the rabbits. She freed them as gently and as quickly as she could, though they scratched her in their panic to get away. She would have liked to pet them, to relieve their distress, but they were wild and in pain. All they wanted was to flee.

As the last rabbit disappeared in the undergrowth, the wolf urged Dana to hurry.

"The hunters will return! They will bring their weapons!"

She was right. Dana had no sooner climbed onto the wolf's

back than the first poacher crashed back to the campsite, toting a rifle.

A shot rang out. Dana screamed. In a grey blur of motion, the wolf charged away.

CHAPTER FIFTEEN

"ARE YOU HURT?" DANA cried. "Are you all right?"

They had cleared the forest and reached the road. The sounds of pursuit died out behind them. Dana slid from the wolf's back. The grey fur was wet with blood.

"It is a graze," the wolf said mildly, licking her wound. "His drunkenness threw off his aim. We had best keep going, little cub. The shadow is on the move. I sense it near us."

"I wish you'd explain—" Dana began, but she stopped in mid-sentence.

She had spotted a car parked at the side of the road. She knew the vehicle. It belonged to Mick, the eco-warrior, Big Bob's second-in-command. He sat in the driver's seat, talking as usual on his cellphone. What was he doing so far from the glen?

"That man knows my father!" Dana hissed to the wolf. "He must be out looking for me!"

"We will hide till he leaves," the wolf decided.

They slunk into the ditch at the side of the road.

Dana heard a second car pull up beside Mick's. Doors opened and closed. A search party perhaps? Then she heard the voices, Mick's and another man's she didn't recognize. The stranger spoke first.

"Time's running out on the European grant. The date's set. August first, we move in. Call a meeting, throw a party, whatever. Just create a diversion and get them out of the way."

"It wouldn't be for long," Mick said. "They won't go far from the site."

"Just get them out of the trees. We can have our equipment there in minutes. Once we start felling, they can't stop us."

"What time?" asked Mick.

"Sunset. A bit of shadow will help. We won't be working long. With the first line cut, we'll have won the battle. It'll knock the fight out of them." The stranger let out a short laugh. "You can't put a tree back up when it's down. Right?"

"I'll do my best."

There was a rustle of paper.

"There's no need for that," said Mick. "The company pays me."

"Consider it a bonus. There's a lot of money flying around this job, I can tell you. Might as well take your share."

As soon as the cars drove off, Dana jumped out of the ditch.

"I've got to warn Big Bob and the others! I've got to go back!"

She was shocked when the wolf disagreed.

"We cannot turn back. You have your mission."

"You don't understand!" Dana cried. "If I don't go back, we'll lose the woods! We'll lose the battle!"

The wolf's voice was quiet and deadly serious.

"If you do go back, we may lose the war."

Dana was drawn up short. She stared hard at the wolf, her guardian whom she had come to trust in such a short time.

"It's all much bigger than I think, isn't it? My mission? My message?"

"You are a smart little cub. Clever as a *faol*."

Returning to the mountains, they continued their journey till the hours of the day caught up with them. Twilight descended in a haze of grey. The moon came out to light up their path. Dana knew they would not make Lugnaquillia by nightfall. When she said so to the wolf, her guide agreed.

"It is not to Lugnaquillia I bring you, but to the Vale of the Two Lakes you call Glendalough."

"We can't go there!" Dana exclaimed. "We'll be seen! There'll be crowds of people, tourists and visitors. My dad and I go there sometimes. The place is always packed!"

The wolf's growl was firm.

"Glendalough is the destination of all *peregrini* who quest in these mountains. That is what you are, little wolf, a pilgrim, a wanderer, one who seeks. In Glendalough you will find food and rest and the guidance you need for the next step of your journey."

Dana was uneasy. Aside from her worry about the crowds, something else niggled in the back of her mind. Something she knew about Glendalough but couldn't recall.

The wolf had stopped on a high ridge on a rocky promontory. Nose to the ground, she sniffed around, then let out a bark. There was a cleft in the rock face, the entrance to a cave. She crawled in first and Dana followed after.

The cave was snug and dry and sheltered from the wind. Moonlight seeped through the opening. With her cloak on the ground and the wolf's back to warm her, Dana would get a good night's sleep. But she didn't want to sleep. She was restless and disturbed. Something was wrong.

"Why do I need guidance from Glendalough when I've got you?" she asked the wolf.

She heard the deep sigh in the darkness, felt the warm wolfish breath on her face.

"I will not hide the truth from you. This is a wrong your kind do to their children. Though you ran with the swiftness of the wolf today, still the shadow has caught up with us. We cannot outrun it, we can only outwit it. To protect you, I must do what I can."

Dana's heart tightened with dread. She sat up, put her arms around the wolf's neck.

"What do you mean? What will you have to do?"

The wolf nudged her to the mouth of the cave. They sat together outside, under the cold eye of the moon.

"Each day death strikes," said the wolf, "yet we live forever."

She licked Dana's forehead with her great rasping tongue.

"Let us sing, little cub. Let us sing of joy and catastrophe. Let us sing of life and death."

The wolf threw back her head and howled.

It was a primal cry, wild and intoxicating. A deep rich unending bay that resounded through the mountains. Dana was electrified, as if lightning shot through her. The song of her tribe. The ancestral call. She threw back her head and howled too, throat wide open as the sound poured out like blood.

They howled for ages, singing to the night, singing to life, singing of hope and courage, of fate and longing. When they were finished, peace settled over them. Dana leaned against the wolf. She was tired now but fighting off sleep. Her time with the guardian seemed suddenly precious.

"Do you have cubs?"

"I had. Long ago. Proud sons and daughters who roamed these mountains. The forests were our haven. When the great woods were cleared, our days were numbered as were the days of the Gaelic order. For the trees hid both wolf and rebel.

"Even as your people were brought low, Dana, so too were mine. Humans have always seen us as evil, all your folk tales make us so. Yet we do not prey on men and we rarely fight even amongst ourselves. We live in clans, we care for our young. Our food is deer, birds, fish, insects and berries. But we also like sheep and cattle, and that made us your enemy.

"Government acts were passed to oversee the slaughter. Bounties were set. All over the country, we were killed with spears, guns, traps, snares. The last Irish wolf died at Wolf Hill in the North in the late 1700s. The land is bereft of my kind. We are no more of Ireland."

"But you . . . you're here," Dana murmured.

Her eyes closed. The wolf's tale had lulled her to sleep. As she drifted into darkness, she finally remembered. The thing that nagged at the back of her mind.

The last wolf in Wicklow was killed at Glendalough.

CHAPTER SIXTEEN

They travelled the next morning in a sombre mood. The wolf was silent and stepped with heavy tread. Dana was oppressed by a sense of doom. The day itself was dreary with mist and mizzle. When Dana tried once again to argue against their route, her guide held fast.

"We go where we must, little wolf. We all have our part to play, whether big or small. Each of us is advancing to her transformation."

"But I don't understand what's going on! Why won't you explain? Aren't you supposed to be guiding me?"

The wolf sighed heavily.

"A true guide shows you the way, inspires your steps. She does not walk for you."

With that, the wolf increased her pace. Dana had to hurry to keep up with her. The discussion was over, for now.

They had a long journey to go to reach Glendalough. The

cave where they had spent the night overlooked the lake of Lough Nahanagan. They had yet to cross the wide esker of Camaderry. It was an arduous trek. As the hours passed by, Dana thought to herself that adventures were always more exciting in books. No one mentioned the sore feet, the hunger and thirst, or the mind-numbing monotony.

Eventually Dana noticed a subtle change in the air, nothing she could see or touch. It was as if a curtain had been lifted or a window opened. Everything was suddenly fresh and vibrant. She found she knew things she hadn't known before.

She was walking the old pilgrim's road so many had trod for centuries past. Pilgrims, refugees, exiles and outlaws had all passed this way. Paths from every direction converged on this route, for all roads through these mountains led to one place: the holy Vale of Two Lakes. *Gleann Dá Loch.*

The Monastic City of the western world
Is Glendalough of the Assemblies.

A simple hermit had founded the site in the sixth century AD. *Caoimhín* was his name—Kevin—meaning fair-begotten or beautiful born. It was said he crossed the mountains in the company of an angel. When he came to the hidden valley of Glendalough, he chose to live alone in a cave on the mountainside. He prayed outdoors no matter the weather, with birds perched on his head and shoulders. Word of his holiness slowly spread till people came from far and wide to meet him. First a community, then a monastery, rose on the site. By the tenth century, it was famed throughout the Christendom.

As knowledge of the place seeped into Dana's mind, she saw them: columns of people walking the road alongside her. They followed the stone crosses and carved boulders that lined the way and by which they stopped to eat or rest. Overlapping in time and space, they were unaware of each other: Gaelic chieftains wrapped in long broad cloaks; Victorian ladies in plumed hats leaning out of their carriages; men in the dark woollen suits of the 1950s. Some were on foot. Others travelled in vehicles, from horse-drawn carts to modern cars and buses. Some were barefoot in rough peasant clothing, others wore medieval garb with rosaries dangling from their waists. Layers of pilgrims through layers of time.

When Dana stumbled on a stone, layers of hands reached out to steady her.

She herself walked quietly beside the wolf. The feeling of dread had begun to lessen. She grasped the hope that spurred all pilgrims. Whether young or old, rich or poor, in couples or families or walking alone, travelling on foot or in stylish carriages, even those who tarried by the side of the road—all of these people had the same destination. The same destiny. The feast was laid out and all were welcome at the table.

Thus Dana came with her companion guide and the spirits of thousands of fellow seekers to Glendalough of the two lakes and the seven churches.

It was a magnificent green valley carved out by a glacier and sheltered by mountains. The dark waters of the Upper Lake were white with lilies. The Lower Lake was fringed by a rushy fen. Again, Dana gazed through the strata of time. She could see the earliest huts of the hermit's disciples amidst the stone churches and monks' cells of later construction. Rising above these were the accoutrements of a medieval monastery: cathedral, scriptorium, workshops, tannery, bakery, quarters for monks and accommodation for visitors. The present-day silhouette overshadowed all the others with its Visitors Centre, hotel and souvenir shops that catered to the tourists who roamed the ruins.

Dana was confused by the multifarious images of the place she knew well. She didn't want to enter modern Glendalough as there was too great a chance she might be recognized. Nor did she want to enter its past, for she knew the wolf's death was waiting there.

As if she could read Dana's thoughts, the wolf spoke softly.

"Stand beside the earliest crossroads and ask of the old paths, where is the way to good?"

"I'm afraid." Dana's voice shook. "Not for me but for you. I don't want you to die."

"Listen to me, little wolf. The shadow draws near. You are not ready to face it. A sacrifice is required. I go not to my death but to my resurrection."

Dana threw her arms around the wolf in an attempt to hold her back. She cried like the child she was.

"No, I won't let you! Please don't do this for me! If I had known, I would never have asked for your help."

The wild breath of the wolf warmed her face. The rough tongue rasped her forehead.

"Be of good courage, *a fhaol bhig*, I will always be with you. Not all that is gone is gone forever."

Though Dana clung with all her might, the wolf was stronger. She broke from the child's arms.

"I will not tell you to turn away. Be ready to face all that comes to you. Who's afraid of death? Not I!"

The wolf threw back her head to howl. One last long howl that echoed through the valley. Then she began to run.

And even as she ran, Dana heard the tantivy. The hunting cry at full gallop as it sounded behind her. Then came the baying of the hounds and the wolfhounds.

"NO!" she cried. "NO!"

She stood her ground to block their path, but the hounds passed through her as if she were a ghost. Close behind came the men on horseback, hoisting their guns.

"NO!" Dana cried again.

They too charged past, into the valley in pursuit of the she-wolf.

Her last run was splendid. A streak of grey amidst the green trees. Legs high to paw the air. Eyes glowing like gold. A cry for freedom. The last run of the last wolf of Wicklow.

Now the hounds encircled her and drove her back to the men. Now the lead hunter shouldered his gun.

The shot rang through the mountains. The wolf somersaulted in the air. A spectacular spin against the clear sky.

Then she fell to the ground, dead.

And she who was of the tribe of Faolan let out a death cry as she too leaped into the air and spun like the wolf, then fell to the earth weeping.

CHAPTER SEVENTEEN

Dana lay on the ground, convulsed with weeping. After a time she began to shiver, at first with shock and then with cold. Something soft and wet drifted around her. Snow! In the middle of summer? She sat up in a daze. The valley was bathed in an icy blue light. The mountainsides were cloaked in snow. The faint tracery of small animals, hares and birds, inscribed the ground. A winter's sun shone palely.

All the layers of time had dissipated. The vale was densely wooded, still and lonely. A raven cawed overhead. Sheets of ice rimed the two lakes. The only sign of life was a small fire lit on the shore of the Upper Lake beside a hut of clay and wattles.

Dana let out a cry. The wolf's body had vanished. She ran into the valley, weeping out loud. *Mama, mama.* Lost in sorrow, not knowing what she did, she ran to the place where she had seen the wolf die. At the edge of the lake, beside the fire, she collapsed in despair.

"Where are you?" she wept. "Where have you gone?"

A gentle hand touched her shoulder. Then came a soothing voice.

Hear my cry, O God,
Listen to my prayer,
From the ends of the earth,
I cry unto thee.

When my heart is faint,
Lead me to the rock,
That is higher than I,
For you are my refuge.

Dana looked up. He was a young man, still in his teens, dressed in deer skin, with bare arms and feet. His hair was long and tangled, as was his beard. He looked wild but not in a frightening way. His features were serene. The grey eyes were kind. She knew who he was—the saint of Glendalough.

Kevin spoke to her in Irish.

"*A dheirfiúr bhig,*" he said softly. "My little sister. What has broken your heart?"

"Brother," she said, dissolving into fresh tears. "I have lost my . . ." She searched for the word that best described the wolf and it came to her easily in her mother tongue. ". . . *anamchara.* I have lost my soul-friend."

He helped her up, placed a cool hand on her brow. She was pale and feverish. Though she had only been wandering in the mountains for days, it might have been weeks. All the twists and turns of her strange adventures, the fitful meals, the sleeping rough, had taken their toll. And now she had lost her dear friend and companion. She was completely undone.

Kevin brought her into the hut, which was sparsely furnished but clean and dry. It was for guests, he explained. He himself lived in a cave on the dark side of the lake. He gave her hot broth with goat's cheese and bread, then told her to rest. The bed was a mattress of sweet-smelling rushes. Still in shock, Dana was unable to speak. Kevin asked no questions, but served her gently, the way Gabriel did when she got sick. She burst into tears again. She wanted her dad. She wanted to go home.

"Sleep, little one, it will ease your pain," he promised. "I must go and pray for you."

When Dana slept, she fell into a nightmare. Once again, she ran with the wolf. Hunters and poachers pursued them with guns. A shot rang out. The bullet pierced her flesh. She cried out in her sleep.

Now the young saint entered her dream. *Come, sister wolf, I grant you sanctuary.* He stood at the lakeshore where water lapped on the stones. His arms were open. Dana and the wolf leaped into his embrace. Kevin held them both as they lay dying.

Tá tú ag imeacht ar shlí na fírinne.
You are going on the way of truth.

When Dana woke, there were tears on her face but she felt renewed and refreshed. She walked out of the hut into a sunny afternoon. The snow on the mountains dazzled her sight. She shielded her eyes with her hands. Then she saw him.

Kevin stood waist-deep in the freezing water of the lake. Arms outstretched, eyes closed, he turned his face to the sun.

Fada an lá go sámh
Fada an oíche gan ghruaim
An ghealach, an ghrian, an ghaoth
Moladh duit, a Dhia.

Long is the day with peace
Long is the night without gloom
Thou art the moon, the sun, the wind
I praise you, my God.

As Kevin prayed out loud, ripples broke the surface of the lake. To Dana's horror, a monster rose up, green and scaly, with a serpent's body and a head like a horse. Coiling and curling, it twisted around the saint till they came face to face.

Dana was about to scream, then stopped.

Kevin had opened his eyes to smile at the monster. A beatific smile. Then he leaned towards the serpent to rest his brow against its head. The gesture was as light and affectionate as a kiss. They stayed that way for an infinite heartbeat, a zoomorphic design from an ancient manuscript. Then the monster slid back under the water.

Kevin walked from the lake, making no effort to dry himself despite the chill. His lips were blue, his skin bone-white, but he appeared oblivious to his own discomfort.

118

Dana was stunned by what she had seen.

"The old stories say you defeated the *péist*. That you banished the water snake to the Upper Lake. But it looks like you're friends!"

Kevin laughed, the merry laugh of a young man.

"The truth is twisted in many a tale. I carried the beast upon my back from the Lower Lake to the Upper, not to vanquish him but to keep him out of harm's way. They would have hunted him down and killed him."

The saint gazed over the smooth surface of the water.

"He is something old. Very old. But he is not the Enemy. We are the ones who make him friend or foe."

"I don't understand."

"Each of us has a 'monster' inside. If we banish it to the deep of our minds, it lies there brooding till we cast it out into others and try to kill it in them. Better to make peace with it. For everything monstrous is, at heart, something that needs to be loved."

He looked at Dana gravely.

"You will meet your monster soon, little sister. I cannot save you from it. None of us can be kept from the truth save at the peril of our souls."

Dana shivered.

"The wolf said you would guide me on the next step of my journey. What should I do? How can I fight the Enemy?"

"Make peace with your monster. Then the shadow cannot touch you. And the Enemy's power will lessen in the world."

He smiled apologetically at Dana's lost look.

"Words, words, what use are they? I am too chatty for a hermit! You will learn as you live, little sister. Just follow the greenway."

He walked her beyond the Upper Lake to the Poulanass Waterfall. Directing her westwards, he pointed upwards to the ridge that led out of the valley.

"Climb the cliffs of Derrybawn to the forest of Lugduff. Beyond the woods, you will see at last the peak of Lugnaquillia. You must reach it today, for it is *Lá Lughnasa*."

Dana was halfway up the ridge when she turned to wave a last farewell. Kevin stood below, birds perched on his head and shoulders. When he raised his arms to bless her journey, she was filled with a sense of purpose and mission. First the guardian of the Faolan clan, then the saint of Wicklow County. The gods of her people had truly answered her call. In her heart she accepted what could not be denied: her quest was greater than a message for a king or a wish fulfilled. As she journeyed to her destination, she journeyed towards her destiny.

CHAPTER EIGHTEEN

Dana had almost reached the top of the ridge when she found herself back in her own time. The wilderness around her wavered and changed. She stood on wooden steps bordering the waterfall, surrounded by people.

The usual summer crowds had flocked to Glendalough. Young and old, foreign and Irish, they strolled through the monastic ruins and around the two lakes. Fifteen hundred years later, people still came to Kevin!

Dana looked around her quickly. No one had noticed her arrival. Everyone was staring at the sky with concern. It was turning dark. The clouds roiled like brew in a cauldron. Gusts of wind shook the trees. The air grew cold. As the first splashes of rain fell, the tourists ran for cover, racing down the steps to the hotel and Visitors Centre. Dana ran in the opposite direction, into the forest.

The trees creaked and cracked around her. Branches whipped against each other. The rain lashed down. She pulled up her hood and quickened her pace. This was not good, not good at all. Summer storms in the mountains could be disastrous. Rivers in spate often flooded their banks. She had only that day to reach Lugnaquillia. Was this the Enemy trying to stop her?

Lightning flashed overhead. Dana tried not to panic, but when the first roll of thunder rumbled across the sky, she ran blindly. Briars caught at her cloak. Rain pelted her face. The ground underfoot was wet and slippery. She didn't see the small creature scurry across her path until it was too late. They fell over each other and tumbled in the mud.

Despite the shock of the fall, when Dana saw what had tripped her, she jumped to her feet. A boggle! She seized the rascal and held on tightly while scanning the bushes around her.

"Where are the others? Tell them to leave me alone!"

"You leaves me alone! Why's you grabbing me?"

The voice was the first clue. Higher and lighter. Then the brown fabric. Though sodden like a used tea bag, it was definitely a dress.

"You're a girl!"

"Course I's a girl!" She was obviously offended. "Ivy's my name. Could I be's anything else but a girl?"

Of course she couldn't. Though she had the same funny-shaped body as the boys—big head, flat nose, long neck, webbed feet—she had curls of green hair like fiddlehead fern. And the eyes that were gold in the gloom of the storm had big lashes that made her pretty. She also looked friendly and very bright.

"Let me go," she pleaded with Dana. "I must gets to the Boglands. Before the storm be's worse."

Dana kept her grip on the girl boggle, uncertain what to do. The wind raged around them. They were both soaked to the skin.

"How can I know you won't harm me? The boggles treated me badly the last time we met."

Ivy looked surprised, then concerned.

"What has the boys been doing? Has they been bold? I knew they'd gets up to mischief without us! What has they done to you?"

She looked so sincere and distraught that Dana released her. Ivy didn't run away. She waited for Dana's answer.

"They kidnapped me and when I told them I had a message for King Lugh, they put me down a hole."

"Oh the bad boys! The sillies! They don't knows the story! They's afraid you would wake the king, but he wakes already. I's going to get them. We needs their help."

Ivy's eyes were huge. She looked wild with worry. She was about to say more when something struck her.

"Dids you say you has a message for our king?"

Dana nodded. "I must deliver it today. It's from the High King of Faerie. Lugh is his *tánaiste*."

"This *is* news," murmured Ivy, thinking fast. "Maybe's good news. What to do? What to do?"

Ivy studied Dana's face. What she saw there obviously made up her mind.

"I helps you!"

"Can you get me to Lugnaquillia?"

"I cans. First we takes shelter, then we makes plans. A friend be's near. Old and wise."

It was Dana's turn to decide if she trusted the other. There was certainly something about the boggle she liked. Besides, the storm was getting worse. Both struggled to stay upright in the wind. Dana knew she wouldn't get far alone.

"Okay, I'll go with you."

Holding hands, the two girls hurried through the forest. The storm was whipping itself into a frenzy. The trees bent backwards with the force of the gale. Ivy stopped in front of a great oak as wide as a porch. It was old and hollow. Dana thought they were going to climb inside for shelter, but instead the boggle knocked on the tree. A door appeared in the bark and opened before them.

Dana was surprised to be greeted by someone she knew. It was the little old lady she first met in Bray and then again in the mountains when she set off on her quest. Under the frilly white bonnet, the narrow face had grown more whiskers and was covered with a soft grey hair like down. She wore a bright yellow skirt over long lace petticoats. Her black beaded eyes twinkled merrily.

"We meet again," she said to Dana, as she bustled the girls in out of the rain.

"Mrs Sootie Woodhouse," Ivy introduced her.

The hollow tree was actually a hallway with a coat stand and framed pictures. Steps led underground. Mrs Woodhouse lit a candle and brought them downstairs to a sitting room warmed by a hearth.

Despite all the marvels of her travels, it was this place that delighted Dana the most. All her favourite picture books from when she was little! There were stuffed chairs with cushions in front of the fireplace and a wooden dresser with blue china and brown crockery. Bunches of onions and dried flowers hung from beams on the ceiling. Coloured rugs covered the floor. Bookshelves and tiny paintings graced the walls.

"Oh what a dotey house!" cried Dana. "I could play here all day!"

Mrs Woodhouse scooted them into the bedroom and gave them towels and dressing gowns. Then she hung their wet clothes before the fire to dry. The chamber had a four-poster bed with a patchwork quilt and a wicker chest for linen. A porcelain jug and bowl were perched on a washstand.

Lunch was ready by the time their clothes had dried. It was just as Dana had always imagined when she dreamed of stepping inside her books! On the flowered tablecloth a little feast was laid out: bowls of piping hot chestnut soup with freshly baked rolls and curls of butter; a platter of soft and hard cheeses; and a salad of dandelions, greens and wild strawberries. Sweet things were offered after the savouries: primrose biscuits just out of the oven and still soft inside, poppyseed buns, crab-apple tarts and a blackberry pudding. Dana helped herself to everything.

Throughout the meal, they chatted and laughed, but soon the talk turned to serious matters. Though they were safe and snug far below ground, they could hear the storm raging above them.

"His heart breaks yet again," Mrs Woodhouse sighed sadly. "Will he survive his memories? Will we?"

"Dana brings a message to our king," Ivy informed her. "From the Gentry of Faerie. They has named Lugh *tánaiste*."

Mrs Woodhouse looked pleased. She poured boiling water into the teapot. The smell of peppermint and camomile filled the air.

"Has he work to do? That would be good. Just what he needs to take his mind off his troubles!"

Ivy agreed. "When men's don't work, they gets into mischief."

Dana was surprised. She had come to think of Lugh as an angry king who frightened the boggles. But Ivy and Mrs Woodhouse expressed no fear, only fondness and concern.

"Could you explain what's going on?" she asked, as they cleared off the table and washed the dishes. "Why was Lugh asleep? Why is he waking up? And why does he make storms?!"

"It be's a long story," said Ivy.

"We will tell it as we go," Mrs Woodhouse declared. "We have dallied long enough, girls. It is time to act."

She dried her hands busily on the tea towel. Her nose quivered with zeal.

"If there is a message for the king, it must be delivered. We will take Dana to Lugnaquillia."

Dana donned her long green cloak.

"We should link arms together so no one will get lost or blown away," she suggested.

Mrs Woodhouse laughed.

"We are not going outside, my dear."

She opened a door on the other side of the room. It led to a souterrain.

"*Under hill and under mountain.* That's the fairy way. We'll reach the king by twilight, dry as a bone."

As they made their way through the tunnel, safely sheltered from the storm, Dana heard the tragic tale of the King of the Mountain.

CHAPTER NINETEEN

Once upon a time and for aeons galore, the fairy Kingdom of Wicklow enjoyed a Golden Age. It was ruled by Lugh of the Mountain, Lugh of the Wood, a happy king who was kind and just. He loved nothing more than to feast and dance and make music and merriment. Every evening at twilight, he would lead his troop in cavalcade with gonfalons flying. His marble palace lay deep inside the highest mountain in Wicklow, Lugnaquillia, named after his good self. Lug na Coille. For a long time he reigned alone until one night, as in a dream, his queen arrived.

She fell from the heavens like a burning star. Old as the world, young and beautiful as the day, she was the one for whom he had waited since time began.

It should have been an unending love. They should have lived happily ever after. But tragedy struck. The lovely queen died mysteriously. Some say it was the spell of an ancient enemy. Others, that she returned to the Realm of the Stars. The king was bereft. He went mad with grief, berserk with sorrow. He tore at the sky and clawed at the mountains. Rills turned to rivers, rivers were in spate, trees toppled, fields flooded. The land was awash with his tears. Day after day and night after night, his lamentations flayed the countryside.

Lugh's people were at a loss to help him, for he was inconsolable. Wherever they gathered to shelter from the storms, they spoke of his plight and of their dilemma. Disaster threatened. The mountain bogs were sodden. If the downpour continued, they were likely to explode. A bog-burst. A deluge. Soil and mud and liquid peat would gush down the mountains like molten lava, swamping all in its path. So many would suffer. So much would drown in the King of the Hill's sorrow.

Something had to be done.

Now, as it is known, there are three gifts to fairy music: songs that make you laugh, songs that make you weep and songs that bring the comfort of sleep, and, as it is also known, the girls of the boggle clan have the third gift. In the olden days, when human babies were stolen by the fairies, the girl boggles always sang them lullabies so they wouldn't cry.

Thus it came to pass, in the Kingdom of Wicklow's darkest hour, that the Clan Boggle rose to save the day. They gathered at Lug-naquillia where their king sat weeping on the cairn at the summit of his mountain. The girls kissed his forehead and hushed and shushed him and held his hands as they began to sing. Soon his lids grew heavy, his eyes closed and his head nodded on his chest, free of pain, free of sorrow. The boy boggles formed a chain to carry the king to the vast bog below. There, they laid him face down and rolled a great stone upon his back. When the boys returned to the Boglands, they went alone. The girls stayed behind to sing to Lugh, keeping him in the blessed realm *of sleep. It was the boys who guarded the borders to keep away anyone who might disturb the sleeping giant. For there was no guarantee that once he woke they would be able to lull him to sleep again.*

Once the borders were closed, by Faerie law, all stayed away.

As the sad tale was told—mostly by Mrs Woodhouse, with additions from Ivy and the occasional query from Dana—they travelled through the tunnels that ran under the Wicklow Mountains. The smell of clay and small animals permeated the air. Passageways ran off in every direction. Dana was afraid they would get lost in the labyrinth, but Mrs Woodhouse always knew the way.

Though they journeyed for hours without taking a break, Dana felt neither bored nor tired. The silver nails in her shoes carried her effortlessly. Her companions kept her entertained. From time to time, Mrs Woodhouse would announce their progress. Lugduff fell far behind them, then Conavalla. There was a great turn in the maze as they went around Table Mountain. Once they passed Camenabologue, they were on the last lap to Lugnaquillia.

"So why is the king waking?" Dana asked Ivy. "Did the girls stop singing?"

Ivy shook her head.

"Some dark thing wokes him. We felts it pass by. We tries to put him back to sleep, but you sees by the storms no luck so far."

"A shadow is crossing the land," Dana said softly. "That's part of my message! It's good that the king's awake to hear it. The Lady who sent me says he'll know what to do."

Ivy cried out, as if struck by a blow.

"But he can'ts do anything! He's under the stone! That's why I wents to get the boys! They has to free him. Bog magic binds everything, even the king."

Dana stopped in her tracks. She was trying not to panic, but this was disastrous. What use was her message if the king was trapped?

"Has I done it all wrong?" Ivy's big golden eyes welled with tears. "I be's a bad leader! All is lost because of me. Now we'll never sees our boys again!"

For the first time since Dana met her, the girl boggle looked tiny and helpless. Dana remembered the boy boggles crying for their girls. How much these little people had suffered!

"There, there, sweetling," said Mrs Woodhouse, kindly. She patted Ivy on the shoulder. "As long as you have friends, you should never despair."

The little old woman drew herself up and spoke quickly to Dana.

"Ivy will bring you to the king. No matter what happens, you must give him the message. I will go to the Boglands to collect the boys. I had hoped to guide you to the end of your quest, but we each have our part to play, whether big or small. Be of good courage. *Follow the greenway*."

"But the bogs are miles away!" Dana said, anxiously. "It will take you—"

She was stopped in mid-sentence by a look from Mrs Woodhouse. The black beaded eyes were laughing at her.

"Do you not yet know me, pet? After all the good care you have given my kinfolk . . . your hamsters?"

As soon as Mrs Woodhouse raced down the tunnel, Dana

understood. The skirts and bonnet were shed like leaves from a tree. A tail flounced in the air. A squeak of a laugh echoed behind, as the little grey field mouse disappeared.

CHAPTER TWENTY

LUGNAQUILLIA WAS THE highest mountain in the Wicklow chain. Bound by three cirques carved steeply in its sides, its summit was a lofty plateau wide and flat as a pitch. It commanded a view of the countryside for miles around.

Dana and Ivy reached the top after climbing for hours through a passage that sloped ever upwards. Though they had heard the storm roaring always above them, they were still shocked by its fury when they stepped outside. The rain lashed the mountain and teemed down its sides. Water seethed in the corries like boiling cauldrons. Hurricane winds howled like the Banshee.

Ivy stared in dismay at the devastation. The summit had been flayed by rain till the ground was a mass of mud and puddles.

"This be's the dancing lawn of the Kingdom of Wicklow . . . We holds our parties here in the midsummer nights . . . There's where the bonfire does be lighted . . . We woulds dance in circles . . . We woulds sing and laugh . . . We woulds feast at long tables under the stars."

Dana couldn't imagine the happy scenes Ivy described. The place looked like a battlefield. She tucked the small boggle under her cloak, as they fought against the winds to cross the summit.

Ivy led Dana to the edge of the cirque called the South Prison. Its cliffs curved in the shape of an amphitheatre. On the higher slopes to the west, a saddle of blanket bog lay between Lugnaquillia and the smaller mountain of Slievemaan. Ivy pointed to the bog.

"Can you hears them?"

Through the wails of the storm, under the wind, came a faint ululation. A lament of many voices that was also a lullaby.

"The girl boggles?" said Dana.

"Can you see's them?"

Dana peered at the expanse of bog lost behind a veil of rain.

"I can't see anything! Not in this weather!"

"You see's me," Ivy argued. "You has fairy eyes. Looks harder. Looks deeper."

Dana concentrated even as Ivy urged her. She could barely make out a vague shape in the landscape. The silhouette of a giant sprawled face down in the bog. But she couldn't hold it for long. One minute she saw the king, arms and legs splayed with a great boulder on his back, the next she was staring at patterns of eroded peat topped by a stone cairn. Then she spotted the erratics, rocks dropped at random by glaciers in ages past. They appeared to surround the giant. Dana rubbed her eyes. Saw the girl boggles where they crouched in the rain, miserable but steadfast, still guarding their king.

The giant stirred. His arms and legs flailed as he strove to surface from the deep. Each time he moved, each time he howled, the storm got worse.

The girl boggles cried out loud. At first Dana thought they cried with fear, for they were surely in danger, but then she saw that Ivy wept too.

"Our poor dear king. We can no longer saves him."

Dana frowned. This was all wrong. Like children being responsible for their parents' problems.

"It's not right," she said to Ivy. "He's the king. He's supposed to look after *you*."

"The boys! The boys!" Ivy suddenly shouted.

Below them, the boy boggles scampered onto the field led by a flash of grey fur with the tail of a mouse.

"Mrs Woodhouse!" Dana cheered.

Ignoring the storm, the boys skated over the sodden ground to reach the king where he thrashed and roared. With one great heave, they rolled the stone back. But as the king rose up free and burst out of the bog, the bog itself burst in a brown explosion. Mudslides gushed and rushed down the mountainside to sweep all in their path.

What happened next was like a long slow dream.

In strange oneiric motion, Dana saw Ivy swept from the summit, saw her drown with the other boggles in the torrent that coursed through the valley. There was no time to cry or mourn. Dana herself was engulfed, buried in a murky mirage of the deep bog and the secrets it concealed. Layer after layer churned to the surface, an upheaval of all that had passed through the ages: primeval forests and long-lost fields; the whitened bones of giant elks and aurochs; the tortured shapes of human bodies, corded and torqued like black bog oak. Celtic gold that was the wealth of kings and the pelf of thieves swirled past like litter: great brooches, coiled torcs, gorgets and armbands, golden shrine boxes, bells and jewelled mitres. The bog was the repository of ancestral memory. Shade and shape fled past like the stages of life.

Above the holocaust stood the king, a dark giant raving against the heavens.

Like a fossil caught in the bog herself, Dana was petrified by this world's apocalypse. Yet she knew she must act. In the midst of the chaos, she hung on to her mission like a candle in the dark. She would do what she had come to do.

David facing Goliath, she cried out to the king.

"You must stop this right now! I have a message for you!"

Now occurred the strangest thing of all in that strange brown nightmare. The king's dark eyes settled on Dana and in that instant, he was suddenly calm. Her presence was clearly a shock that jolted him out of his madness. He thrust his great fist into the bog to grasp her where she floundered. Then the wind went still, the rain ceased, the storm died.

Dana was standing on the summit of Lugnaquillia.

Before her was a young man with craggy features and dark-brown skin. He looked nothing like the giant freed from the stone. His manner was quiet, his blue eyes serene. He appeared to be in his teens, but the shadow of grief made him older and wiser. His clothes were earth colours, green and brown, and he wore a purple mantle. The golden circle that bound his dark hair was the only sign of his kingship.

"Who are you?" he demanded. "How came you here?"

He sounded astonished but not crazed or angry. Dana was relieved. She paused for breath, held her head high. All her adventures had brought her to this moment.

"I am Dana Faolan of the County Wicklow. I bear a message for you from the High King of Faerie."

Before King Lugh could respond, Dana spoke her mind. She could feel her knees shaking, but she had to say it.

"This is all your fault!"

She waved her arm to take in the great ruts and hollows in the mountain, the bog blown asunder, the landscape deluged.

"It's not fair to make everyone suffer just because you're unhappy. The poor little boggles who did so much to help you! And Mrs Woodhouse and all the animals—" She choked back her tears. She had never been so sad or so angry. "I won't give you the message till you put everything back where it was. You're the king. I know you can do it."

She expected him to erupt. She feared he might unleash more storms. Instead, the sorrow in his features deepened. His look was both grave and stern.

"Do you really care for my people, human child? Then prove your love."

His voice was quiet, but as his words sank in, Dana recoiled as if he had shouted.

"It is the feast of *Lá Lughnasa*. The day on which I can grant any boon. I will restore my land and people . . . if you *wish* me to do so."

CHAPTER TWENTY-ONE

D ANA WANTED TO SCREAM.
It wasn't right! It wasn't fair! After all her hard work, her days and
nights on the road, her trials and mishaps. She was to give up her
wish? Her hopes and dreams? Her last chance for happiness?

She could easily refuse. She had the best excuse. The wish
was really for Gabriel. After all her dad had suffered, it was only
fair. She tried not to think of Ivy and Mrs Woodhouse. Were
they alive or dead? What if she were their only chance for survival? Tears streamed down her face. It was too much to ask.
She was too young to be called on to make such a sacrifice. To
give up all hope of finding her mother, restoring her family and
staying in Ireland. To give up the very reason she had come on
the quest!

"I can't do it," she whispered.

A light breeze warmed her face, like gamey breath. In her
mind, she saw the wolf before her, golden eyes shining.

"Whether big or small, we all have our part to play, little cub."

The wolf's image changed to that of Saint Kevin. His gaze was steady.

"When my heart is faint, lead me to the rock that is higher than I."

Dana couldn't escape the truth. She was part of something greater than her own needs and desires. Two worlds were involved and so many lives. How could she think and act just for herself?

"I wish . . . that you restore your kingdom."

Her voice quavered as she spoke, but she forged ahead.

"I wish that you put everyone and everything back where they were before the bog burst."

The king's face shone like the sun after a storm. Admiration rang in his voice.

"You have done what the best of mortals do. You have sacrificed yourself for the rescue of Fairyland."

He raised his arms. His cloak billowed behind him. The golden circle on his brow flashed like lightning. He was a giant again, proud and powerful. The King of the Mountain. Lugh of the Wood. He began to sing in a beautiful language that sounded like music and bird song and water falling. He was chanting and enchanting the land.

It was like a film in reverse. Everything that had been swept away flew back to its place: soil, water, mud, river, flora and fauna, boggle and fairy. Every bird was in its tree, every fish in its stream. The Kingdom of Wicklow was returned to its glory.

Lugnaquillia shone in the half-light of a beautiful evening. The air was fresh after the rains. The sweet smell of drying grasses wafted on the breeze. The summit was a smooth sward of heather and deergrass. Peeping out were all sorts of mushrooms—golden Honey, viscid Slippery Jack and nut-brown Pennybun. On the north-facing crags, a flock of ravens settled into their nests as the first bats emerged for their evening feed.

The sun was setting in the Glen of Imaal. A rose-coloured glow lit up the western slopes of Lugnaquillia. A hush lay over the landscape, silvered with the tracery of rain. Lugh drew a sweeping arc in the air. In response to his gesture, a rainbow swept across the sky. He raised an eyebrow to Dana as if to say *good enough?*

Before Dana could react, Ivy stood beside her, looking bright and cheerful in a rose-petalled dress. The boggle grinned at her friend, but turned immediately to the king to drop a curtsey. The other girl boggles came racing up the slope. They all fell on Lugh, like apple blossoms from a tree, kissing his hands and hugging his knees.

"You's well, dear king?"

"We needs not sing no more?"

He gathered them up like an armful of flowers and planted kisses on each as they squealed and giggled.

"My thanks to you, ever-loyal boggles. You have done more for your king than he would ever have asked."

When he put them down, they gathered around their leader, Ivy.

"We goes home now? Home to the boys?"

The boy boggles were still climbing the mountain when the king shooed the girls away. They met each other halfway on

143

the hillside. There were hugs and whoops and somersaults of joy, laughing and singing and screeches of happiness. Then they all set off together to return to the Boglands.

Ivy remained behind, reluctant to desert Dana.

"Does you want me to stay with you?"

Dana shook her head. She knew what it was like to be homesick. She was suddenly feeling that way herself.

"You go home. You deserve it. I just hope we'll meet again."

"Will we meets again?" Ivy demanded of Lugh.

He smiled down at the boggle leader.

"Bravest of boggles, you will surely meet your friend again. Your king gives his word."

That was all she needed. With a big hug for Dana and a hoot to the others, Ivy was off to catch up with the last stragglers heading east.

Lugh sighed to see them go, already missing their high spirits, but there was work to be done.

"Now for my message, little one," he said to Dana. "All kings and princes look to the High King. What does the *Ard Rí* say to me?"

The evening had grown cooler as the sun set in the west. Like the boggles, Dana yearned to go home. She was tired and dispirited. Though she had accomplished her mission, her dream was shattered. She knew the message was important, but not to her. Great events were afoot in the Realm of Faerie, the concern of kings and queens. She had played her small part. There was nothing left but to say the words and return to her father, empty-handed.

Lugh simply nodded when she told him he had been named the *tánaiste*. Then she gave him the message.

A shadow is crossing the land. The Enemy rises. Where is the light to bridge the darkness?

The king strode back and forth, deep in thought.

"Even as I lay dreaming, I felt the shadow darken the land. It was this which woke me. Though I was loath to wake, still my royal duty called."

Dana wasn't really listening. She was wondering if Lugh would take her home or if she would have to make her way back through the mountains alone. Her heart sank at the thought of another long trek. She started to sniffle. Nothing had turned out the way she wanted. Tears began to fall.

The king snapped out of his thoughts. He stood before Dana and tipped her chin.

"Why do you weep?"

"Because I'll never find what I'm looking for."

There was amusement in Lugh's eyes as well as sympathy, the response of an adult who knows more than the child.

"All you have lost is a wish, little one. That does not mean I cannot help you."

A strange hungry look crossed his features.

"What has brought you to me, Dana Faolan? What is it you seek?"

"I . . . I want . . . to find my mum."

Again that hungry look in his face but so much fiercer now, it made her nervous.

"Your mother is missing! For how long is this?"

"She left when I was three, just over seven years ago."

"I have slept too long," he murmured. His voice was shaking. "This is why you are here. Only you could find her and only I could show you the way."

Dana was bewildered by his words but overjoyed as well. All she really understood was that her dream had been revived.

"I'll go right now!" she declared.

"Not now," he said, "but soon. You are not yet ready. You do not know the story. Tonight you will stay in my palace under the mountain. In the morning, you will set out to find your mother."

He had no sooner spoken than they were inside the mountain, in a fabulous hall glittering with light. The floor was green marble, the walls were crystal. Music sweetened the air like perfume.

"Stay by my side," he advised her, "and no harm will befall you. Say nothing of the marvels you are about to see or you will break the enchantment that allows you to join us. As you are under my protection, you may eat and drink."

A shining company peopled the hall—the fairy lords and ladies of the Kingdom of Wicklow. In rich garments adorned with jewels, they stood in silence, looking warily at the king. A gentleman stepped forward, silver-haired, in a cloak of green leaves. Slung over his shoulder was a golden harp.

"Hail Lugh of the Mountain, Lugh of the Wood. Helpless and hapless, we have waited for thee. Art thou well, my king? Hast thou returned to thy people?"

Lugh smiled upon his harper and all his courtiers, all fey and immortal with sad and glad eyes.

"I heard you weeping as I lay in slumber, your hearts broken with mine. Dear companions, I am truly restored."

Cheers resounded through the hall, a tumultuous welcome for the return of the king. Out of thin air, a banquet appeared and the bright assembly took their seats. Lugh extended his arm to guide Dana to the table.

"But I'm not dressed—" she panicked, then she let out a gasp.

Her muddy clothes had transformed to a gown of blue silk with a silver shawl. Diamonds sparkled at her ears and throat. Her dark curls were caught up in a jewelled comb. She swished her dress with delight and took the king's arm.

At the head of the table, two golden chairs stood side by side like thrones. Dana was surprised when Lugh led her to one as he took the other. His court was also taken aback. Though everyone glanced curiously at her, the mystery of her presence was left unexplained.

As the feast commenced, Dana helped herself to every dish. The food was heavenly. Everything melted in her mouth or burst on her tongue. There were terrines of chilled dill soup and hot soup of almond, stuffed pumpkins garnished with cranberry sauce, sweet-potato pie, asparagus soufflé, savoury cheese-and-onion tartlets, and hearts of artichoke vinaigrette. She was already eyeing the desserts, which included ginger sherbet and apple pudding, lemon ices, apricot mousse, choco-late custard and fruit ambrosia.

While the others talked and laughed together, Dana ate without speaking. Throughout the meal, she was dogged by the oddest impression. *Nothing was as it seemed.* She was acutely aware of some unseen web that held this fragile world together. *Fairy glamour.* Any awkward questions or statements of disbelief could tear the delicate cloth asunder.

Despite her care, from time to time, it unravelled anyway. She was about to bite a peach coated in chocolate when she saw the huge wild berry she held in her hand. She blinked. The peach returned. Sometimes the swaths of lace and diamonds turned to spider webs stippled with dew. The greatest confusion had to do with size. There were times when she felt like a giantess dining with titans in the hall of the gods. Then again, she sat at a table with other tiny creatures, all fitting snugly inside a rabbit hole!

Dealing with the strange nature of fairy reality was only part of Dana's trouble. The unease in the hall was palpable. It ran like a dark stream beneath the bubbles of merriment. She sensed the courtiers were holding their breath. What did they fear? What could possibly happen?

The king himself was preoccupied and brooding. Head in hand, he sat without eating. Occasionally he would heave a deep sigh. Towards the end of the banquet, when Dana had consumed more than her fair share of desserts, he stood up to make his announcement.

"My harper will tell it!"

The feasting came to a halt.

"Tell what, my Lord?" the others cried.

They gasped in horror at his reply.

"Tell the tale of my woe."

Chapter Twenty-Two

Silence had fallen over the hall. The bright lords and ladies looked aghast. None would gainsay their king, but all obviously feared he might go mad again.

The first strums of the golden-stringed harp issued notes so sad and exquisite that Dana's eyes welled up with tears. A longing seared through her. Only the gentle press of Lugh's hand on her arm stopped her from crying out. In some inexplicable way, deep in her heart, she knew the tune though she couldn't imagine where she might have heard it before. It had all the power and vagueness of a lost but persistent dream or a mother's random humming to soothe a child to sleep.

She didn't have long to dwell on the music's mystery as a new marvel followed. The magic of fairy storytelling. Once the harper began to sing, Dana found herself inside the tale with sight and sound and scent.

Once upon a time, there lived a king who ruled from Lugnaquillia in the heart of Wicklow. Strong and just, merry and kind was Lugh of the Mountain, Lugh of the Wood.

Aeons passed. Seasons changed. Snow melted on the mountains. Rivers burbled in the thaw.

"Will you not marry?" chirmed the birds.

"Will you not take a wife?" hummed the bees.

The king let out a great laugh. It was the same question each spring and he gave the same answer.

"I am waiting," he would say. "She will come."

One Midsummer Feast she arrived at last, falling from the heavens like a burning star. She landed by the bonfire he had lit on the summit. He had just made his wish, the same wish he whispered to the flames each year: let her come to me now.

She had travelled far. She was confused and afraid. But when her eyes met his, she remembered why she had come.

"Are you the King of the Morning?" she said.

"If you are the Queen of the Day," he replied.

"Are you the King of the Evening?" she bade.

"If you are the Queen of the Night," he sighed.

"Will we dance all summer long?"

"We would pass the time in pleasure."

"Will your love hold full and strong?"

"You would be my treasure."

She was a speirbhean, a skywoman, with hair pale like moonlight. She was one of that tribe who herd the white stars across the heavens each night. Having fallen to earth, she kept her light cupped in the palms of her hands.

They were wed in the autumn when the leaves clothed the ground with a red-and-gold carpet. The festivities went on for a year and a day. Forever young, forever beautiful, they danced on the summer lawns of Lugnaquillia. They rode the night skies on the cool lunar winds. They sang in their winter palace on the Murrough by the sea. Their love was as boundless as the waters that bordered their realm. As strong and free as the winds that rushed down their mountains. As warm and as gentle as their green fertile valleys.

When they fought, as couples do, tears and storms flooded the low-lands. When they reconciled, the sky spilled over with arcs of rainbows.

Dana was so captivated by the romance of the tale, she forgot she was viewing a tragedy. She was not ready when it came, not ready at all.

One bright spring day, the fairy queen went a-maying. She and her ladies tripped lightly through the woods, gathering blossoms of whitethorn to weave in their hair. When her companions sat down to a picnic of seed-cakes and honey, the queen didn't stop. She was chasing two butterflies, a holly blue and a silver fritillary. They were getting the best of her in a game of hide-and-seek. She pursued them through an old forest, over the ridge of a mountain, down into a steep glen wooded with oak and ash. She was aware of the grey road far below, where mortals drove their noisy vehicles, but having little commerce with humans, she chose to ignore it.

The queen found the blue hiding in a holly tree and was about to hunt out the fritillary when she heard the music.

It drifted on the air—high silvery notes, dipping, gliding, fluttering like the very butterfly she sought. Head cocked on her shoulder, eyes closed to listen, she was caught by the sound. A bewitching melody. Like nothing she had ever heard before. She edged closer, keeping always to the shelter of the trees as she travelled downhill to the source of the sound. She was nearing the road, the human road, but she couldn't resist the music. So strange, so beguiling, so . . . earthly.

When she came to a clearing, halfway down the woody slope, she hid behind an old tree. Her hair was snarled by prickles of holly. Red berries hung from her ears and around her throat like rubies. She peered through the leaves to gaze on the young man who commanded the glade.

He was dark-haired with a tangle of curls that framed a handsome face. His eyes were as green as the sea, his skin tanned brown. His body was slender, bowed like a branch as he strained over his music. He pressed his lips to the silver flute to serenade the trees as if they inspired him. At first the tune was slow and yearning, then it changed to wild trills like birds in flight.

She was charmed by what she heard and saw. She was enchanted by the music and the man.

At first she hummed along with his tune, then she began to sing. Like silver thread embroidering cloth, her voice entwined itself inside his music. It took him a while to discern the sound, but as soon as he did, he stopped playing his flute. She continued to sing as he stood entranced, listening and looking and finally locating where she was.

He spied a pale and beautiful face in a cluster of leaves. Fair hair tangled with holly, eyes like blue stars. His heart tightened. For the first time in his young life, he fell madly, deeply, hopelessly in love.

She stopped singing when she realized he had found her. She was about to flee when he called out, called out with love and yearning. She was doubly caught now.

Shyly, she stepped from the shadows of the trees into the sunlight. She wore a gown of green silk. Her arms and feet were bare. Her hair shone like pale gold, wreathed in whitethorn. She trod softly towards him on white hind's feet that barely touched the ground.

He was stunned by this vision of a glimmering girl.

They stared long at each other, fairy and mortal. Both did not really know what the other was. Both were lost in a spell of love and forgetting.

At last he smiled. He had a musician's heart, as wild as the hearts of birds.

"I thought it's bad luck to pick hawthorn in May," he said. "I was told it's the flower of the fairy queen. The flower of the White Goddess."

She threw back her head and laughed. The sound shot through him like quicksilver. His soul was scalded. His blood was afire. He wanted to hear that laugh again and again.

"Your speech is strange to me," she said. Her voice was mellifluous. "Are you of Ireland?"

"I'm Canadian," he replied. "Of Irish descent. I've come over for the year, to collect tunes and work with local musicians. I'm a composer."

"Gabha an cheoil." She clapped her hands with delight.

He was captivated.

"'A smith of music,'" he repeated in English. "What a great title."

"You speak the language of your ancestors?"

"Tá mé a foghlaim. That's another reason I'm here. To brush up on the teanga. I'm learning it at college back home, but I want to be fluent. This is the place to do it, eh? The old sod. The holy ground."

They sat together on a fallen tree. They spoke in Irish. He played her some of his compositions. She sang along. He made changes to suit her rhythms so that new tunes were forged, tunes that were both human and fairy, tunes that were woven with new love.

She walked out of the Glen of the Downs that day, hand in hand, with her mortal lover. He didn't return to his homeland. She didn't return to hers.

As the last strain of the harp resounded through the marbled hall, Dana found the courage to meet King Lugh's eyes. She hadn't recognized the fairy queen at first, but she knew the young musician immediately. With great love and great pain, she had watched the tale of her parents' union unfold.

And it was with great love and great pain that Lugh now gazed upon Dana. Great love, because she was the daughter of his beloved queen and had some of her features. Great pain, because it was her birth that sealed the doom of his loss.

"Thus you have heard," he told her, "the fairy tale that is called *The Wooing of Edane.*"

Dana shivered to hear her mother's name said with such significance and sorrow and awe.

"I searched the mountains for my queen when she did not return. In my heart I knew some terrible thing had happened. The death of winter was in the air. Though I sought far and wide, she was not to be found in the Land of Faerie.

"Months passed before my troop brought me word of her fate. We had not thought to seek her in the mortal realm. It was only by chance that she was seen in the woods and only by chance, indeed, that she was recognized. For she wore a human guise and no longer appeared fairy.

"I hastened to the home of this man, furious and wrathful. I would strike him down, take back my wife. But alas, though I stood before Edane as her rightful husband, she did not know me. Under a spell of love and forgetting, she had wed her mortal lover. What is more—and this, I knew, would seal our doom and keep us parted—she carried his child."

It was such a sad story that Dana wept with the king whose wife had been stolen by her father. She could see how all parties were innocent and how all had suffered.

At the same time, she couldn't help but feel a ray of gladness. A surge of relief. Now she knew for certain: it *wasn't* her fault. It wasn't some flaw of hers that had driven her mother away and broken her father's heart.

"She must have remembered," Dana said softly. "That's why she left. She must have remembered."

As the truth dawned on the fairy queen's daughter, a new question arose.

Where was she now?

CHAPTER TWENTY-THREE

The following day, Dana stood on the summit of Lugnaquillia. She had woken that morning in a silken bedchamber, overwhelmed with excitement. *Today she would find her mother.*

Beside Dana stood King Lugh. In the short time she had known him she had come to like him, despite the conflict of loyalties and the final twist in the tale. There would be no reunion of Dana's parents, no return to the family of her hopes and dreams. Her mother wasn't human but a fairy queen and Edane's true husband was the King of the Mountain. With the innate sense of justice all children have, Dana knew it had to be this way. But it wasn't easy. She couldn't help but be sad for herself and her father.

As if he knew her thoughts, the king spoke quietly.

"You might have been my child, Dana. I shall always regard you as my stepdaughter in the other world. Will you think of me as your fairy godfather?"

Dana burst into a grin.

"I like it! Are you coming with me?"

Lugh shook his head. "This is your quest, your mission. Only you can find her. You are the child of her heart, blood of her blood." He looked towards the east. "Alas, I have other duties this day."

That's when Dana remembered. In the rush of events, it had slipped her mind.

"The Glen of the Downs! The traitor Mick! Did they cut the trees?"

"The trees still stand," Lugh told her. "Because of the storms. But they will be felled today, at twilight."

"You'll fight it, of course?" said Dana. "With fairy magic?"

"Only humanity can fight the Enemy. If your race fails to stand against the shadow, we of Faerie must withdraw before it."

Dana was shocked. And confounded.

"Honor said you would know what to do once I gave you the message! Why—?"

Her eyes widened as the pieces of the puzzle suddenly clicked together.

"The message!" she cried.

A shadow is crossing the land. The Enemy rises. Where is the light to bridge the darkness?

At last she understood. Why she was chosen for the mission. Why the High King insisted she was the one.

"My message! My mission! My search for my mother! *They're all connected!* She is the light that will bridge the darkness! I've got to find her, not only for you and me, but for Faerie as well!"

The king smiled at her proudly.

"You are ready, little daughter."

He led her in a wide circle round the rim of the summit. They went slowly as if on a ritual walk. When they reached the broad saddle between Lugnaquillia and Slievemaan, Lugh stopped and pointed the way.

"Slievemaan," Dana murmured. "*Sliabh na mban*. The Women's Mountain."

As they said their farewells, Lugh grew concerned.

"The shadow has haunted you throughout your quest. It will surely rise against you as you seek the light. I cannot follow where you go. Can you protect yourself?"

Dana spoke slowly. "A holy man told me if I made peace with my monster, the shadow would have no power over me." She shrugged. "But I'm not sure what he meant. I don't know what my monster is . . ."

Lugh put his hands on her shoulders as if hoping to instil his strength in her. "The monster within is part of the shadow without. You will know when it rises. Be of good courage, little daughter, and you will fare well. *Follow the greenway*."

Cloak whirling behind her, dark curls blowing in the wind, Dana set off bravely to the Women's Mountain. She was nervous and excited and also afraid, but mostly she was consumed by one thought: *I'm going to find my mother, I'm going to meet her at last*.

She stopped once to wave to the king. Half-lost in the clouds settling over the mountain, he stood like a giant against the sky. Then he was gone, her last companion.

Loneliness crept in like the mist. Dana knew in her heart it was now all up to her. She had nothing but her own strength and experience to guide her. For when a girl goes out to seek the Great Mother, no one may go with her, no one can help. It is a sacred quest, an inner journey, that she makes alone.

The mist seeped everywhere, shrouding the landscape, curling at her feet. Dana moved slowly through the silent shadows. Time and space seemed awry. She lost any sense of day or night. She was walking in the Wicklow Mountains and yet she wasn't.

She was lost in an abysmal place of flying forms and dark spaces. There was no sound, no light, no warmth. She was searching for something. In the distance there was movement. She drew near to what looked like a mountain. On the peak was the dim shape of a house. The door opened and a child's pram, painted black, rolled out. Over the edge of the cliff it tipped, then it sped crazily down the hillside. A woman stood watching. Had she let it go? Had she pushed it? Now the pram was a stone rolling onwards. Now the woman was a tree, twisted and alone.

Dana clenched her fists. She recognized her nightmare, pushed it away. To bolster her courage, she tried to imagine the wolf padding beside her. But the image wouldn't hold. Nothing held in this place. Though her fear was growing, she did not turn back. She would not give up. Half-fairy, half-mortal, this was her birthright. To walk between the worlds.

It seemed ages before Dana saw a dim light ahead. Slowly moving towards her, it swayed back and forth. At last she made out a hooded figure carrying a lantern and leading a donkey with laden baskets.

By the time the person reached her, Dana had given up trying to discern its gender. The features kept wavering, one minute feminine, the next male. Nor could she get a clear impression of gender itself, for the masculine face might appear gentle and kind, while the female was fierce and raging, then again the male looked cruel while the feminine softened. In the end Dana had to accept that this person was both male and female and somehow neither.

"Who are you?" Dana demanded.

She was glad to hear her own voice. A good solid sound. She had begun to feel like a ghost in the mist.

"I am the Chronicler. What do you seek?"

"I'm looking for my mother."

The Chronicler pointed to the donkey's panniers. They were filled to the brim like treasure chests, not with jewels, but with books.

"You may choose one."

The situation was too bizarre to question. It had the same relentless logic of a dream.

Tentatively Dana touched one book and then another, attracted to all the different kinds and colours. There were paper scrolls and Egyptian papyri, tablets of wax and clay, manuscripts of vellum, hand-sewn texts bound in calfskin, some even inscribed on thin sheets of gold. There were modern books printed with glossy covers as well as talking books, computer disks and videotapes. A metallic box that glowed and hummed contained strange unrecognizable devices: laser, electronic and holographic books which Dana surmised belonged to the future.

Some of the works she knew, while others were a mystery. *The Book of Time. The Book of Names. The Red Book of Ormond. The Yellow Book of Leccan. The Book of the Dun Cow. The Book of Lindisfarne. The Mahabharata. The Mabinogion. The Books of Mica Schist.*

The Book of the Dead. The Book of the Living. The Book of Dreams.

She picked one whose title caught her eye. *The Book of Childhood.* The cover showed a great river flowing under a stone bridge. There were hundreds, no thousands, maybe millions of children gathered on the riverbanks. All were drinking the water. Some drank from cracked cups, others from their bare hands.

Dana was mesmerized by the image.

"What does it mean?" she asked the Chronicler.

"The river is the inexhaustible source of life. The children who drink from cracked cups were loved from birth. For though the cup is flawed, as with all human love, still it is a gift that helps to nourish them. The children who drink from their own hands were not given love. They must help themselves to the river of life."

"How sad," murmured Dana.

"The saddest tale of all," said the Chronicler.

Dana thought to herself that while things hadn't been perfect, at least she'd got a cup.

She reached next for *The Book of Dreams* but it was taken from her.

"Not yet. It is a tale to be told in your future."

By this time Dana was almost on top of the donkey, digging into the baskets for buried treasure. Here was the world at her fingertips! Everything she ever wanted to know at a glance! Her arms were full of exciting books about dinosaurs, myths and the creation of the universe. She was about to grab more, when she stopped. She could be there forever. Lost in thoughts. Was this a trick? A test? A trap? She tossed the books back.

"You must choose one," the Chronicler repeated.

In exasperation, as only a child would do, Dana closed her eyes and dug into the pile. She pulled out a book with blank covers.

"How about this one?"

The Book of Obscured Memories.

Inside the deep cowl, the Chronicler's features changed. The gentle face of Saint Kevin looked out at Dana.

"'Obscured' means secret or hidden away, little sister. Memories may be obscured for good reason. Before you look into the book, take heed and take care. *I cannot save you from it. None of us can be kept from the truth except at the peril of our souls.*"

Dana was suddenly afraid. More afraid than she had ever been throughout the quest. She had been caught off guard. She wasn't ready. She couldn't have known it would come this way. So subtle. So sinister. Yet here it was. The challenge of the shadow.

Something stirred inside her, deep in the abyss, some monstrous memory she had buried long ago. Everything inside her screamed: *Put the book aside! Leave it shut! Don't look!*

Dana was quaking so hard she thought she would faint. Like a small child waking in the dark alone, she faced the terror of the unknown. She wanted to hide in the covers. She wanted to scream for her dad.

She steeled herself. She refused to hide. If she had to do this to find her mother, then do it she would.

Dana opened the book.

163

CHAPTER TWENTY-FOUR

THE BOOK OF OBSCURED
Memories began where *The Wooing of Edane* had ended.

The young musician and his beautiful wife moved into a little cottage in the Glen of the Downs, not far from the place where they first met. The young bride had to be near the woods and mountains for she could not bear the town or crowded places. A year later, their child was born. A sweet-natured baby with her father's dark hair, she had her mother's eyes that shone like blue stars.

Not yet twenty, Gabriel worked hard to support his family. He taught music in the town, busked in the streets, and played on the bandshell at the seafront in the summer. They didn't need a lot of money for they lived simply and their rent was small. Edane made a pretty human, dressed in floppy hats and brightly coloured clothes. Her favourite place was the garden. Everything she grew flourished—fruits and vegetables to eat, flowers to enjoy. Their home was filled with light and music, love and laughter.

From time to time something odd would happen.

The baby was only six months old when Edane laid her on a blanket on the grass in the garden. The leaves of a young ash tree sheltered the infant while flickering with sunlight to keep her entertained. Back in the kitchen, the mother, as she baked, watched her child from the window. She turned for a moment to put the pie in the oven and when she looked back, she let out a scream. The baby was surrounded by wild animals. A fox licked her face. The badger was nudging her out of a damp spot. Birds flitted above her to make her giggle. As soon as Edane cried out, they ran away but not without casting reproachful looks at their queen who had forgotten them.

Another time Edane woke at night with a mother's instinct to glance quickly over at her daughter's cradle. She heard muffled laughter, saw lights glimmering above the child. Half asleep, her sight hazy, she caught but a glimpse of luminous wings. She gasped. They vanished.

Dana observed her mother's reactions, how she ignored or denied what she saw, how quickly she forgot. The spell of humanity was woven so thickly around her, it repelled anything that threatened to unravel it.

Now Dana saw herself as a three-year-old toddler.

Stocky and strong-limbed with bunches of dark curls, she was curious and courageous, a mischievous little girl. She would run away from her parents, try to climb trees, chase the chickens and kittens around the garden. No longer a baby, she was becoming herself, discovering who and what she might be.

One day she cupped her hands together and let out a whoop. With peals of laughter and delight, she ran to her mother to proudly offer the prize. A pool of golden light welled in her palms.

Edane's face distorted. Memory tore like a knife through the spell that bound her. In horror, she backed away from the child who carried her mark, the sign of the Light-Bearer. She backed away from her child as she remembered who she was, as she remembered her true life and the king she had forsaken. She backed away from her child as her mind and spirit broke.

With the force of a blow, Dana remembered that moment. The shock. The agony. The severing of the cord between mother and child. From deep inside, the monster rose.

It was *something you did. You* are *the reason your mother left.* You *are the one who broke your father's heart. It was* you *who tore your family apart.*

Dana dropped the book as if it burned her. A cry tore from her throat, from her heart. She ran away from the Chronicler, away from the truth, down the mountain, stumbling blindly.

Far in the mountains, a child was lost. Out of the mists she ran and across the bogs, weeping out loud. She ran without purpose, cold face to the wind, sodden feet sinking into muddy ground, her child's heart as wild as the hearts of birds, shattered like an egg that had fallen from the nest. Her cries mingled with the lament of the sheep that scattered before her. *Maammaaaa. Maammaaa.* The serpent coiled inside her mind, squeezing and strangling.

It was your fault. You are to blame. You are the monster at the heart of your family.

Was it for hours or days that she ran? She stumbled through the rain and drizzle, out of the mountains and into the foothills, past a derelict cottage with broken windows and a tangled garden, down over a ridge that led into a glen severed by a road. Dimly she recognized where she was and slowly returned to herself.

The tree houses in the Glen of the Downs hung askew like ruined nests. Battered by the storms of the previous day, they had yet to be repaired. The site was deserted. Led by their betrayer, Mick, the eco-warriors were at the far side of the glen, dismantling a bulldozer left to distract them. Big Bob patrolled the trees alone. There was little fear of a raid. It was almost sunset. No one worked in the dark.

As twilight descended over the valley, the shadows in the forest deepened.

Now Dana saw what the eco-warriors couldn't see. In the silence of the evening, bulldozers advanced on the glen like a line of tanks of an invading army. Behind them came the trucks that bore the chainsaws, the iron machinery of progress and war.

With her fairy eyes, Dana also saw the refugees who were leaving the glen. On a height above the road, a shining figure, King Lugh called his people to their mountain sanctuary. Birds, small animals, the watery sprites of the stream, the spirits of the trees and flowers, all fled the destruction of their home. As Dana witnessed the exodus, images flashed through her mind. Similar scenes she had seen on television. Lines of the homeless, displaced or expelled, trudging hot roads or through frozen forests, children and old people, weeping women, all driven before the onslaught of the shadow.

As the first iron blade sliced through the bole of a tree, Dana's fairy blood quivered. Sharp teeth sawed through the wood. A young oak fell. Red sap seeped from the bloodied stump. More trees were surrounded, more crashed to the earth. A dimness settled over the valley, as life and light were being extinguished.

Big Bob came running as soon as he heard the chainsaws. He knew immediately that he had been betrayed. Sickened, defeated, he made his last stand by an old beech, as the trees fell around him like soldiers on the battlefield.

At the slaughter of the trees, Dana's fairy self woke. Lightning shot through the silver blood in her veins. She let out a cry of protest that echoed across the glen and over the mountains, a cry from a human child with a fairy soul, a cry of rage and grief for the Mother Earth.

MAMA!

She looked down at her hands. Ever since that fatal day, she had refused to let it happen. She had denied her gift. In that one searing moment, she had learned to hate it, to banish it forever to the depths of her mind.

Now the monster rose up from the lake of her mind and Dana saw that it was beautiful and shining with light. She smiled with love at the gift of her birthright. She bowed her head to acknowledge its beauty.

If you make peace with your monster, the shadow cannot touch you. And the Enemy's power will lessen in the world.

Dana cupped her hands together. As the light welled in her palms, she raised them to the sky in offering.

The light shone like a beacon to cross the worlds, to reach the one who was lost in darkness, who had heard her cry but couldn't answer, who now saw the light and ran to meet it.

A giantess came running out of the west and over the mountains, glimmering hair streaming behind her. In her palms, she cupped a light.

On the eastern ridge, Dana's hands spilled over to suffuse the sky with an arc of light. When the giantess stopped on the western ridge, her light poured forth to join with Dana's.

Beneath the shining bridge of light, the Glen of the Downs lit up like day.

The Enemy works best undercover in darkness, in secret and silence, through furtive action, covert operations and clandestine relations, when no one is certain, where no one can see. Who can fight shadows? What is being fought?

In the broad light of day, the motorists passing through the glen couldn't help but see. Images too stark to be denied. Ancient trees falling. Chainsaws cutting. Bulldozers ploughing great ruts in the earth. One man alone, arms around an old beech, face wet with tears.

They all knew about the protest. Many were against it. They wanted the road widened so they could drive faster. They didn't care about trees or nature or the life of the valley.

But there were others who supported the tree people, who had made contributions, signed endless petitions. They saw Big Bob standing alone and they knew in their hearts it was time to act. Whether big or small, they had a part to play.

A silver Mercedes screeched to the side of the road. A middle-aged businessman jumped out. He ran to the nearest tree that was about to be felled and put his arms round it. He placed his body between the bark and the blade.

A secretary on her lunch break pulled up in a red sports car. She ignored the mud on her high heels as she picked her tree and ran to protect it.

Now a local builder taking his kids for a drive saw the others guarding their trees. He stopped his van—"For Outdoor Work, I'm Your Man"—and he and his three children tumbled out. He stood in front of a bulldozer holding one little girl in his arms, while the older two stood on each side of him like warrior-princesses.

More and more drivers pulled into the shoulder when they saw what was happening. A human chain of defence quickly formed round the trees.

Following the light that shone over the glen like a star, the eco-warriors hurried back to their camp. In an instant, they joined the fray, shinning up trunks like squirrels and swinging on ropes from branch to branch. Cheers and war cries resounded through the valley.

In the distance, sirens wailed. Police cars soon converged on the site, followed closely by news reporters. The developers knew they had lost. Their work came to a halt.

Only vaguely aware of events below, Dana waited on the ridge as the shining figure drew near. Too impossibly young to be anyone's mother, she was no longer a giantess but a shy slender woman with long pale hair and eyes like blue stars. She looked at Dana as one who had hungered and thirsted for such a sight.

"Mama?" Dana whispered.

Dana knew her but didn't know her. She was the mother

the baby dimly remembered, but she hadn't aged with the years. Still apparently in her teens, she didn't look like a "mum." Dana was quaking inside. She heard her mother murmur. *Child of my heart, blood of my blood.* Dana longed to go to her, to be touched and held, but she couldn't move—she was cold and stiff.

"Why did you leave me? Where did you go?"

The words had been frozen so long inside her, they were as sharp as ice picks.

Tears welled in the blue fairy eyes of her mother. Pain marred her beauty.

"I was lost, my little one. I fell between the worlds. Between those I loved in one and he whom I loved in the other. I have wandered for years in the darkness unable to find my way out."

"You were lost in the dark?"

Disbelief edged Dana's voice. Old anger rose up, the unappeasable rage against a mother who had abandoned her child.

"How could you be lost in the dark? You carry the light!"

Her mother held out her hands as if to plead, but also to offer. The light streamed from her palms like a fountain. Without thinking, Dana lifted her hands to catch the flow. It was the same movement she had made years ago. Once again her own light shone there.

"Don't you see, my daughter?" Edane said softly. "I lost the light when I lost you."

Dana could hold back no longer. She ran to her mother. As she was clasped in an embrace that the worlds would never break again, she understood at last.

"I am the Light-Bearer," her mother whispered. "You are the Light that I bore."

CHAPTER TWENTY-FIVE

LUGNAQUILLIA WAS LIT UP like a millennium cake with a thousand candles. Banners and flags fluttered in the breeze. A great silken pavilion was pitched on the summit. Banquet tables with snow-white linen were laden with a lavish feast. Bright fountains sprayed elderflower champagne. Dark fountains splashed red cranberry wine. There was music and dancing, juggling and acrobatics. Games and races were played on the hillsides: hide-and-seek in the starry saxifrage, tag in the lady's mantle, high jumps over St. Patrick's cabbage.

All the denizens of the Kingdom of Wicklow in all the forms of the land of Faerie were present: elegant lords and ladies with melodious voices, miniature moth-like beings streaming gold dust behind them, brown boggles and blue boggarts, tall columns of light, the birds of the air and the beasts of the forest. All creatures great and small, all beings bright and beautiful, had come to join in the celebration.

Standing in the midst of the joyous crowd was Lugh of the Mountain, Lugh of the Wood. Resplendent in the greens of hill and forest, his face shone like the sun. He saw nothing and no one but the Lady of Light who stepped as if in his dreams towards him.

She too was lost in a dream come true. She flew into his arms like a bird who has journeyed far to find shelter at last in the lee of the mountain.

"My love, my only love," they murmured to each other.

Dana had arrived with Edane only moments before, but was already feeling out of place. She wanted to go home. Home to her dad.

"Here you is! I hopes you be here!"

Ivy was fancily dressed in a skirt of bluebells with a necklace and earrings of lapis lazuli. Dana was so overjoyed to see the little boggle that she picked her up like a favourite doll and swung her around.

"I'm so glad you're here! Can you help me get home?"

"Go home? You can'ts go home! You's the star! You's the hero. This be your homecoming party!"

"What?!"

Before Ivy could explain, a silence had fallen over the gathering. King Lugh was speaking.

"Pleasant it is, dear friends, to meet once again on the dancing lawns of summer after the longest winter our kingdom has ever known. This is a day of great jubilation. My Lady and I are reunited and a battle has been won in the heart of the woods. There is one we must thank for this wondrous tide of events."

Dana nearly died of embarrassment as all eyes turned towards her. Both the king and queen smiled at her with love, but Lugh raised his hand before applause broke out.

"Yet it is not we who shall give her praise and thanks but honoured guests who come to our table. Give welcome, my people, to the High King and High Queen of Faerie."

The horns of Elfland rang out. *Taratantara.* A fatamorgana of sound that swelled over the mountain. Bands of multi-coloured flame exploded in the sky like fireworks as a great dolmen took shape like an arch.

"There'll be talk of UFOs over the Wicklow Hills tomorrow," Dana whispered to Ivy.

"You's for what?" hissed Ivy, but she kept her eyes on the shining portal.

When their High Majesties stepped through at last, Dana was amazed to discover she knew the two of them. The High King over all kings was none other than the young man she had met in the glen, the one who first told her to *follow the greenway*. Dressed in black like the night, with red-gold hair to his shoulders, he bore a glittering star on his brow.

It was the young woman beside him who most startled Dana. No longer the pretty teenager betwixt and between, Honor looked every bit the High Queen in her shining raiment and jewelled crown. Solemn and regal, she addressed the throng.

"Glad we are that Lugh of Wicklow is restored to his kingdom. Glad we are that the Light-Bearer is returned to the Summer Land. A battle has been won today, in the heart of the woods, in the hearts of humanity. And yet more fair tidings we bring to thee."

A thrilled hush fell over the crowd as they waited to hear the good news. Only Dana was uneasy. Something pressed so insistently inside her, she could hardly breathe. Some huge nameless thing she couldn't remember. Her heart beat wildly like the heart of a bird, as the High King spoke.

"Today the mortals saved the woods. As it has always been since time began, it is humanity who must come to the rescue of Fairyland. It is humanity who must fight the shadows of the Enemy. We have many champions in the human realm whom we call our friends. But know this and rejoice, my people. One more powerful than all the rest has entered the two worlds."

The child part of Dana was ready to run. Down the steep slope and onto the road and back to Bray. Far far away from the grand destiny that called her.

Edane stepped forward with a high proud look.

"I am the Light-Bearer who bore the Light. *Where is the Light that will bridge the darkness?*"

Dana didn't run.

Her mission in the mountains had prepared her for this moment. Her quest had been her training. Her search was for herself. Inside her, the wolf threw back its head and howled. The monster rose from the deep to rest its head against her brow. As the crowds parted before her, cheering and calling her name, she took her place amongst kings and queens.

The High King raised his arms.

"In the name of Dana Faolan ní Edane, let the festivities resume!"

As the party got underway with even wilder abandon, Dana turned to Honor with a slight air of reproach.

"You're the High Queen of Faerie!"

"Yeah, can you believe it?"

Honor burst out laughing.

"Did you know all the time, then? Who my mother was? That I—"

"I did and I didn't," Honor rushed to explain. "Honestly, I kept forgetting. I was betwixt and between, sometimes human, sometimes fairy. Midir—the High King, my husband—he knew, of course, he knows everything, well, almost everything, but then he's been around for millennia or more. The point is, it was better that I didn't know. It let us get around the rules. That's how I was able to help you." Honor shrugged. "Desperate times call for desperate measures."

She reached for a tray of fairy buns.

"Here, try these. They're yum. Those are flakes of gold. You can eat them."

Dana couldn't resist the cakes or Honor's good humour. They were giggling and laughing when Edane joined them.

Her mother planted a light kiss on Dana's forehead.

"My daughter, of whom I am so proud."

Dana smiled at her shyly. It would take time before she could accept this young woman as her "mum." She had already decided to call her by name as she usually did with Gabriel.

"I've got to go home," she told her mother. "I don't want to just yet, but Gabe must be out of his mind by now. It's not fair to him and I really miss him."

Edane put her arm around her daughter.

"You will be returned to your father soon. It has already

been arranged. While we revel here, no time will pass in the Earthworld. This is your feast, Dana—enjoy it."

And enjoy herself she did. She danced with boggles and fairies, frolicked with foxes and hares, sang with the wild birds who nested on the crags and rolled down the hillsides with parties of pixies. She twirled in wild dancing circles, kicking up her legs and clasping hands with all her new friends and family, now Ivy, then Edane, now Honor, then Lugh. She tasted most of the sweetmeats and treats that were offered in abundance: hazelnut meringue, cranberry rhubarb sparkle, marbled peaches and cream, apple-blackberry pie, blueberry jelly, spiced carroty nutcake and sugar-glazed raspberries and strawberries dipped in chocolate.

Only when the party began to wane was Dana called into the silken pavilion. There sat the High King on embroidered cushions. To his left was Honor, his queen, and to his right was his *tánaiste*, Lugh. Beside Lugh was Edane, who rose to join her daughter. All looked pleased but serious, as if they had just held a council.

"Is it time to go?" Dana asked. She took her mother's hand. "Will I see you—?"

"Often," Edane promised. "Nothing will keep us apart again."

"Before you leave," the High King told her, "we must advise you. Because of who and what you are, you will be drawn again into our affairs."

"You are not alone in the Earthworld," Lugh explained. "We wish you to join with our other mortal friends."

"One of them is my twin sister," Honor said eagerly. "You'll recognize her right away. She looks just like me. In my human form, that is."

"You will have to leave Ireland," Edane said gently, "and travel to a country across the great ocean. It is the land of your father's—"

"Oh!" said Dana. "*Canada?* Is that the place you mean? What a coincidence!"

She saw them recoil, a slight shock on their faces. Only Honor understood and muffled a snicker.

"There's no such thing as coincidence in Faerie," she said quickly to Dana. "It's kind of like swearing to say that word. Actually, it's blasphemy."

"Oh," said Dana again, "sorry. But am I right about Canada?"

"Yes," they all agreed.

Thus on the day that the Light-Bearer's daughter accepted her destiny, she accepted also her new destination.

CHAPTER TWENTY-SIX

THE GLEN OF THE DOWNS
was ablaze with sunset. The sky glowed in washes of red and
gold. The landscape had a rosy hue. The public protest had
ended. The day was won. Even as the national news reported
the events, the road developers withdrew their equipment. The
surprise tactics had failed and a long struggle in the courts
loomed ahead.

"I was never one of you," Mick said to Big Bob with a
shrug. "Companies pay me to infiltrate groups like
yours—unions, radicals . . . It's a living."

"While your soul is dying." Big Bob's eyes were sad. He had
liked and trusted this man. "If you win, you lose, Mick. It's your
birthright, too, that we're fighting to protect."

Mick spat on the ground, then left the site.

The eco-warriors climbed back into the trees to repair their
houses, to resume their watch. A few stragglers still hovered

about but most of the people who had joined the protest had gone home, pleased with the part they had played that day. A lone police car remained in the area.

Gabriel drove through the glen on his way into the mountains for yet another search. With him was Aradhana, who had stayed by his side since his daughter's disappearance. He stopped the car near the campsite to check in with Big Bob. The eco-warriors were taking turns to help look for Dana. As he walked from the parking lot, Gabriel happened by chance to glance at a spot halfway up the ridge. A spot he had managed to avoid seeing for many years, having convinced himself it no longer existed.

His heart quickened, he caught his breath. Light glimmered in the trees as if a star had fallen there. Gabriel told himself it was probably a flashlight, one of the tree people patrolling on high, but he had to be sure. Aradhana also saw the light and, though she couldn't know what it meant to Gabriel, she saw the fierce flash of hope in his eyes. She hurried after him as he clambered up the slope.

It was a steep climb and the ground was sodden from the storms but Gabriel knew the way, knew exactly where he was going. As he neared the spot, his breath caught in his chest, his heart ached. He hardly dared to hope. *Please let it be*, he prayed. And then he saw her.

There in the clearing, where the ancient oak withdrew to form a fairy circle, where the holly curled over the trees like a tangle of green hair, there by a fallen tree trunk stood his daughter.

Dana waved shyly.

Still in the shadows, Gabriel stood stunned. There was something wrong, something weird and disturbing. A pale light shone around his daughter, making her a ghostly figure. By some trick of perspective, she seemed as tall as the trees. She wore a green cloak and flowers in her hair.

"Can you see her?" Gabriel hissed to Aradhana.

He was beginning to fear he was falling apart. Half-crazed from his need to find Dana, was he hallucinating this vision of her? He was seized with a paralysis of mind and body. He was *fairy struck*.

Aradhana frowned at the glimmering girl. Such marvels were not unknown amongst her people.

"I see her," Aradhana said firmly. "Go to your daughter. Bring her home."

It was all the urging Gabriel needed. The fairy spell broke. Even as he ran towards Dana, the light around her dimmed. She looked more solid and of normal size.

As her father ran towards her, Dana saw the toll the past days had taken on him. His clothes were scruffy, stubble covered his head and chin, his eyes were red from weeping and swollen from lack of sleep. Fear and despair had nearly destroyed him, her dear beloved dad who had raised her on his own and always done his best to make her happy.

Dana was suddenly a little girl who had endured a great deal.

"DADDY!" she cried. *"MY DADDY!"*

And she ran like the wind into his arms.

He gathered her up, weeping and kissing her and crushing her against him, holding her so tightly she might never get away again.

"This is the place, isn't it, Dad?" she whispered to him.

He looked around. Everything blurred through his tears but he knew what she meant. He had known it the minute he saw the light in the trees.

"Yes," he said softly. "This is where I met your mother."

And as he looked towards the very spot from where she had stepped twelve years before, Edane entered the clearing. As with the first impression of Dana, she appeared as tall as the trees. Then her form diminished to human size, but she still shone like a star that had fallen to earth. Forever young, forever beautiful, she had not changed since the day he met her.

As he gazed upon her, Gabriel finally accepted what he had always known but could not admit. His wife did not belong to this world. She was one of the other race who dwelled in Ireland.

The blue fairy eyes regarded him solemnly yet the look was distant. She was no longer bound by the spell of mortality.

"I regret the pain I have caused you, Gabriel Faolan. It was not my wish and I have suffered too."

Her voice was silvery like the music of his flute. He was already thinking of her as a beautiful air that belonged to his past.

"I thank thee for the great gift of our child," she finished.

"The great gift you gave me also," Gabriel replied.

They smiled at each other as the last strains of their song came to an end.

Still clinging to her father, Dana reached out to clasp her mother. For that one moment, suspended between the two pillars of her creation, Dana's life was perfect. Though they would not live happily ever after together, they would all live happily.

❖

"I cannot stay," Edane said at last, kissing her daughter goodbye. "We shall meet again."

In the shadow of the trees, cloaked in green leaves, a fairy king waited.

Now Aradhana stepped into the clearing. She had stayed back as she witnessed the family reunion. But when she saw the shining woman depart, she went to Gabriel and Dana and took their hands. The three walked out of the Glen of the Downs together.

The last police car was just about to leave, when the driver recognized Gabriel and the young girl beside him.

"Isn't that the missing kid?" he said to his partner.

They got out of their car.

"Did the eco-warriors—?" the first policeman began, but Gabriel hurried to explain.

"It had nothing to do with them. It was . . ." He racked his brain, thinking fast, then realized that the truth was best. "She was with her mother's people."

The policemen exchanged looks. Just as the sergeant suspected. It was often a family matter, these child disappearances.

"Do you want to press charges?"

"No," said Gabriel, with a wry smile. "We'll just have to work out custody arrangements."

Dana and Gabriel grinned at each other as they walked with Aradhana back to the Triumph.

"Are you okay, kiddo?"

"Couldn't be better, Gabe."

Epilogue

T HE THRILL OF FLYING! A
rush of wings and wind, blue spread of sky, white tufts of
cloud streaked with sunlight. Upwards, ever upwards as the
world falls away!

It was as wonderful as Dana had ever imagined. Below her
lay Ireland like a great rumpled cloth cast out upon the glimmering sea. A patchwork quilt of greens and yellows threaded
with the silver of ancient rivers. She felt a surge of love for her
mother-country and looked again at the land with fairy eyes.
There was the she-wolf crossing the plain. Saint Kevin in his
cave by the Glen of Two Lakes. The boggles racing sheep
through the Sally Gap. King Lugh and Queen Edane on the
peak of Lugnaquillia.

Follow the greenway.

"Dad, this is brilliant!"

Gabriel grinned. Dana's face was pressed to the airplane

window as she gazed out, entranced. He too was overflowing with happiness. Like daybreak after the darkest hour, so many good things had happened since Dana's return. One of the biggest surprises was her whole-hearted acceptance of the move to Canada.

"What about . . . your mother?"

"She wants me to go. She'll be there too."

Gabriel asked no more questions. Dana offered no more details. It wasn't going to be easy, but they had already reached an understanding. He would not interfere with her connection to Faerie while she would keep its effect on their lives to a minimum. One thing was agreed for certain: she would *never* go away again without his permission.

Their situation was eased by the help of a third party.

"Gods, *devas*, angels, fairies, they are all part of life," was Aradhana's view. "This can be hard for people to accept if they have square minds."

"Are you calling me a blockhead?!" Gabriel had protested, laughing.

She had become an indispensable part of their little family. It was Dana who urged Gabriel to ask her to marry him.

"It's not that I haven't thought about it," Gabriel said. "I can't stop thinking about it. But with all these big changes, all at the same time—you and your mother, over to Canada, my family, my new job, your new school—could we really take on a wife and stepmother on top of it all?!"

"Gabe, when you put it that way—do you really think we could do it without her! Do you want to?"

Dana leaned across her father to nudge Aradhana, who was

reading the airline magazine. Despite the last-minute booking, they had been lucky, getting three seats in a row.

"Did you remember to bring your camera? Suresh wants photographs, not postcards, for the kitchen bulletin board. To go beside the ones of India."

"He's going to miss you so badly," Gabriel said with a pang of guilt.

"He can come and visit whenever he likes. He will have lots more money now that he owns the whole restaurant," Aradhana pointed out. "Besides, he will see me at the wedding."

"I hope you won't regret your decision. Your whole life will be different."

Gabriel took her hand and pressed it to his lips.

"You swept me off my feet," she said. "Where I come from, that is what suitors are supposed to do."

As the two laughed and joked together, Dana went back to her window-gazing. They had moved out over the Atlantic Ocean. The great dark waves heaved below in ponderous slow motion. Life was so strange. Things had not turned out at all the way she had hoped, yet she was happy. Very happy.

And her future shone ahead of her like a star over Canada.

GLOSSARY

Tá grian gheal an tsamhraidh ag damhsa ar mo theach. (taw gree-on gyal an sour-oo egg dow-soo air mo hee-ach) — The summer sun is dancing on the roof of my house.

Fáilte romhat. (fawl-cheh row't) — You're welcome.

tánaiste (tawn-ish-ta) — Tanist, second-in-command, heir presumptive; in modern Ireland this is the title of the Deputy Prime Minister, second in line to *An Taoiseach* (awn tee-shock), the Prime Minister.

Is breá an tráthnóna é. (iss braw awn traw-no-na ey, as in "hey") — It's a fine evening.

'Sea. ('shah) — It is, yes. Abbreviated form of *is ea* (iss ah), meaning "it is."

*Conas tá tú, a mháthair? (*cawn-us taw too, ah waw-her?) — How are you, mother? It is an old and courteous custom to use "mother" or "father" when addressing the elderly.

mo stór (moh store) — my treasure

Éist nóiméad. (aysht mo-made) — Listen a minute.

Go raibh míle maith agat. (go rev meela mawh a-gut) — Thanks a million. (Literally, "May you have a thousand thanks.")

a chara (ah har-ah) — my friend, my dear (vocative)

gruagach (grew-ah-gawk) — hairy goblin (perhaps from *gruaig,* meaning "hair"), ogre, giant, fearful warrior, champion

Bean Nighe (ban knee) — Washerwoman, i.e. a fairy washer-woman

Bean Sídhe (ban shee) — banshee (literally, "Woman of the Sidhe," i.e. woman of the Faerie Folk)

bogach (baw-gawk) — soft ground

pollach (powl-awk) — hollow place, from *poll* (powl), meaning "hole."

Lá Lughnasa or *Lá Lúnasa* (law loo-na-saw) — August first, Lammas. Named after the Irish god Lugh.

faol (fwale) — wolf. Literary, archaic word. In modern Irish, the more common usage for "wolf" is *mactíre* (mock cheer-ah) literally "son of the land."

Faolán (fwale-on) — a derivative of *faol,* meaning "wolf." Clan or family name anglicized to Whelan, Whalen, Phelan, Phalen. Also spelled O'Faoláin.

Gleann Dá Loch (glown daw lock) — vale of two lakes

Caoimhín (quee-veen) — Kevin

a fhaol bhig (ah ale vigg) — little wolf (vocative)

a dheirfiúr bhig (ah greh-fur vigg) — little sister (vocative) *anamchara* (ah-nam kara) — soul friend

Tá tú ag imeacht ar shlí na fírínne. (taw too egg immy-acht
air shlee nah fearing-uh) — You are going on the way
of truth. This is a literal translation of the phrase
Irish-speakers use to refer to the dead. They will say *Tá sí
ag imithe ar shlí na fírínne* (taw shee ag immy-heh air
shlee nah fearing-uh) — She is gone on the way of truth
— to say "She is dead."

Fada an lá go sámh
Fada an oíche gan ghruaim
An ghealach, an ghrian, an ghaoth
Moladh duit, a Dhia.

(fawdah awn law go sawve
fawdah awn ee-huh gawn groo-um
awn gya-luck, awn gree-un, awn gwee
muhla dit, ah yee-ah)

Long is the day with peace
Long is the night without gloom
Thou art the moon, the sun, the wind
I praise you, my God.

péist (paysht) — fabulous beast, reptile, snake, worm, monster

Lug na Coille (lew nah kwilla) — Lugh of the Wood

Ard Rí (ard ree) — High King

speirbhean (speer-van) — skywoman, a type of fairy

gabha an cheoil (gaw-vah awn kee-ole) — smith of music

Tá mé a foghlaim. (taw may awh folum) — I'm learning it.

teanga (tang-ah) — tongue, language

Sliabh na mban (shleeve nah mawn) — the Women's Mountain

ní (knee) — abbreviated form of *iníon le* (in-een leh), meaning "daughter of." Hence, Dana ní Edane is Dana, daughter of Edane.